J.B.
TURNER

GONE BAD

A Jon Reznick Novella

NO WAY BACK
P R E S S

Published by No Way Back Press

Copyright © 2010, 2013, 2016, 2017 J.B. Turner

Cover Design by Stuart Bache
Typeset by Couper Street Type Co.

ISBN: 978-1-9997541-1-2

PRAISE FOR J.B. TURNER

"J.B. Turner knows how to put together a great thriller...a great addition to the thriller genre, with all the necessary ingredients required to deliver the goods: tension, drama, thrills and a cast of tough, no-nonsense characters."

Shots Magazine

"Turner has written a book which combines the paranoid conspiracy of Three Days of the Condor with the relentless action of the Reacher thrillers."

Crime Fiction Lover

"JB Turner has really done it...A sensational story."

Tracey Lampley, *Book Mistress*

"Powerful mix of politics, corruption, soap opera, racism, terrorism and sexism."

Eurocrime

"A high-octane tale of international intrigue."
Daily Record

"This is a top class thriller – it ticks all the boxes of the genre: high-stakes plot, fast paced action, intriguing political conundrums – all of which combine to make it a real page turner."
Mark Gartside, Author of *What Will Survive*

"This book pulls no punches. Every action or in–action adds to a chain of events that keeps on gathering pace. This is a hard-nosed investigative thriller that left me wanting more."
Tony's Thoughts Book Blog

"Well plotted and paced, with an engaging cast thrust into believable circumstances…it looks to be a cracking series."
Oz Noir

"The deeper you get into the story, the web of secrets, lies and cover ups and their reveals builds tension and adds drama…A great addition to any crime fiction fans' bookshelves."
Bookshelf Butterfly

To Susan

The car crossed the state line just after midnight.

Hunter Cain shifted in the passenger seat as he dragged hard on a cigarette. He stared out as the headlights pierced the dark Florida highway.

"How long till we hit the diner?" he asked.

The driver cleared his throat. "Twenty minutes."

Cain stared straight. "You wanna step on it?"

The driver nodded.

The miles flew by. He counted down the minutes in his head. The more he thought of what lay ahead, the crazier he felt.

The neon-lit diner came into view and the driver pulled up beside a Chevy pick-up. They went inside and sat down in a corner booth.

Cain looked around. A couple of grizzly trucker types, an old man reading a paper at the counter, country music in the background. The waitress approached and smiled. "Hi guys. What can I get you?"

Cain ordered scrambled eggs, toast, black coffee and pancakes. The driver ordered hash browns and strong coffee. The waitress smiled. He waited a few moments till she was out of earshot. "I appreciate your help with this, bro."

The driver smiled. "Forget it."

A few minutes later the waitress returned with their order. "Here you go, guys."

Cain ate his food. It was the best food he'd tasted in more than eight long years. He waited till the waitress left them alone. "Are they expecting me?"

"Oh yeah." The driver grinned as he ate his hash browns.

Cain's gaze wandered round the diner for a few moments. He finished his food as the place slowly emptied. It wasn't long till it was just Cain, the driver, a waitress and the black short-order cook he could see in the back.

"Feeling better?" the driver asked.

Cain nodded.

The driver used his tongue to prize some food out from between his front teeth. He got to his feet and cocked his head in the direction of the bathroom. "Gonna take a leak before we head off. Be a minute."

Cain said nothing. He watched the driver head through the swing doors to the bathroom. Took a few moments to compose himself. Felt the plans were coming together. In fact, felt crazier than he had for a long, long time. He took a deep breath and headed to the bathroom.

Pushed open the doors and went inside. No one in the stalls.

The driver stood at the urinal and turned round. "Last stop till we get you out of sight."

Cain walked toward the man. He pulled a knife out of his back pocket and thrust it hard into the driver's carotid artery. He collapsed in a pool of blood, gurgling for life.

Cain kneeled down. Liked what he saw. The man's eyes were filled with tears as he bled out on the tile floor. "Nothing personal, bro. Just the way it is."

Then he stabbed the driver through the heart. Again and again.

ONE

Late in a near-deserted New York dive bar. Jon Reznick was listening to a job offer as he drank draft beer out of a Styrofoam cup. His friend and old Delta buddy, Brad Jameson, leaned in close as they sat on stools at Jeremy's Ale House, a few blocks from Wall Street.

"You need to think about this, man," Jameson said. "It's right up your street."

Reznick glanced at his watch and sighed. Had to catch an early flight from JFK.

"Jon, I'm telling you," – Jameson was leaning in close – "guy like you'll make a goddamn fortune in the Middle East."

Reznick zoned out as he stole a glance at the rerun of a Giants game on the TV. Gulped the rest of his beer.

"Purely advisory role … high six-figure sum for eighteen months' work."

"I don't know."

"What don't you know?"

Reznick grabbed another cold beer and leaned

5

on the bar. "I've kinda moved away from that sort of stuff, Brad. It's not really what I do."

"Here's where I'm at, Jon. Three clients are asking for the same thing."

"Foreign governments, you mean."

"Sort of … in a roundabout way."

"So I'd be discussing strategies with these foreign-government advisers?"

Jameson leaned in close. "High six figures, man. Year and a half and you're home and dry. And here's the thing – my firm has some pretty kick-ass financial accountants who take care of our business. We work it so you pay zero tax."

Reznick nodded. The money Jameson was talking about was very tempting. But he knew it meant being based overseas, undoubtedly in some shithole like Riyadh.

Jameson leaned in closer. "I'll arrange it so we get you a phenomenal apartment, gated community, pool, and I absolutely fucking guarantee … absolutely fucking guarantee that you get a crazy generous expense account. I don't think I'd be lying to say you'd clear a million bucks, all in, for one stint. You won't have to spend a dime. And you get the money transferred to whatever account in whatever country you want."

"Tell me some more about this client. This government."

Jameson cleared his throat and leaned in close. "Qatar. They're getting a helluva reputation."

"Too hot."

Jameson closed his eyes and gulped some beer. "Are you fucking kidding, Jon? Too hot? Man, you've been in Somalia. Now that was fucking hot, right?"

Reznick glanced up at the TV showing a slow-motion touchdown replay.

"You wanna know who'll be with you?"

"I don't know, man."

"We got six SAS signed up, four Delta …"

"Who?"

"You won't know them. Left in the last year. After us. But I've checked them out. Top-drawer, man. Keen. Young."

"That's ten. Eleven if you count me."

"Three ex-Navy SEALs."

"Fourteen. That it?"

"Pretty much."

Reznick glugged the rest of his beer. "I'll think about it."

"Jon, I need you there, man. My eyes and ears."

"Said I'll think about it."

Jameson grinned and put his business card in Reznick's pocket. "I live three blocks from here. You wanna talk about this later today, before you head home, or if you've got any queries, don't hesitate to call, you hear me?"

Reznick said nothing.

"Hey, you wanna crash at my place? Angela won't mind."

"I've already booked into a place off Times Square."

Jameson showed his hands. "Hey, just a suggestion. Don't want to cramp your style …"

Reznick said nothing.

"Jon, look, I'm sorry I didn't keep in touch."

"Forget it."

"You know how it is. You get involved in stuff, before you know it, it's like, where the fuck has the time gone."

Reznick smiled. "Tell me about it."

Jameson stared at him long and hard. "You're miles away, man."

"Been a long day. Flight down from Maine and all that. Got an early start."

Out of the corner of his eye Reznick saw two guys enter the bar. Dark suits, white shirts and tight-knotted ties. He recognized them immediately. One was speaking into a cellphone, both looking in his direction.

Reznick said, "Two interesting characters at the door."

Jameson glanced sideways. "Hedge fund kids from Wall Street?"

Reznick shook his head. "Don't think so."

Jameson stole another sideways glance. "I see what you mean. Interesting."

The two men were walking up to Reznick and his friend.

Jameson said, "Think we're gonna have company."

Reznick said nothing.

The two men looked at Reznick. The taller one, behind, stared down at him. "We need you to come with us, sir."

Jameson turned round and snarled. "Who the fuck are you?"

Reznick held up his hand to quieten his former Delta colleague. "No problem. I know these guys."

Jameson said, "You sure?"

Reznick nodded. "I got your card, Brad. I'll be in touch."

"Jon, are you okay there?"

Reznick shrugged and got off his stool. "What do you think?"

Jameson grinned and lifted his bottle of beer. "Catch you round, Jon. And phone, goddamit." He stepped forward and hugged Reznick. "I love you, man. This is a serious offer. Think about it."

"I will." Reznick extricated himself from Jameson's bear-like grip and followed the two men out into the steamy New York air. Parked right outside was a black SUV.

The back door opened. FBI Assistant Director Martha Meyerstein stared out.

"Sorry to cut your night short, Jon. We got a problem."

TWO

The car pulled away and headed along FDR Drive toward uptown Manhattan.

Meyerstein turned and looked at Reznick. "You smell like a goddamn brewery."

Reznick stared straight ahead. "You wanna cut to the chase?"

Meyerstein sighed. "We hope you can help us."

"I don't know … I'm considering heading overseas for a while."

"So I believe."

Reznick smiled. "Roving bug, huh?" he said.

She raised her eyebrows. She knew what he meant. Listening in to cellphone conversations.

"I couldn't possibly comment." Just a hint of irony in her voice.

"I'm serious. I've got a big offer to think over. And I've got to give an answer in the next twenty-four hours."

Meyerstein sighed. "I see."

Reznick shifted in his seat as they sped on. "Where we going? Got a room at the Hilton, Times Square. Need to pick up my gear."

"We'll get that sent on."

Reznick ran a hand through his damp hair. "You got some water?" The driver passed back a bottle of chilled water and Reznick gulped it down.

Meyerstein said, "Like I said, we got a problem. And we're on the clock ourselves."

"So where we headed? Don't know if I'm too keen signing up to a little FBI investigation without knowing more."

The car ran over a pothole and jolted them in their seats.

"A situation's emerging."

"What kind of situation?"

"Anti-government militia leader escaped from a maximum-security prison."

Reznick said nothing.

"I know, it doesn't sound good, but it happened. And we've got intelligence saying there may be a reason for the escape. Pre-planned."

"You mean he got out with inside help, and is planning to carry out some sort of terrorist attack, right?"

"Pretty much in one, yeah."

"So how did he escape?"

"Pulled a toilet from a cell wall and got through a vent in a maintenance tunnel."

"As you do."

Meyerstein rolled her eyes. "Jon, I could do without the sarcasm. I've had it up to here."

Reznick blew out his cheeks. "What have we got on this guy?"

"He's served eight of a twenty-year sentence for planning terrorism. Heads up a Florida militia. Highly trained, highly organized and ruthless. Rumored to have killed bikers, Aryan Brotherhood, blacks, anyone who crosses him. Organizes his militia along paramilitary lines. Divided into cells. Take down one, but you can't take them all. Highly intelligent. Killed a guard last year for, in his words, *looking at me funny*."

"So how do you need my help? Sounds like a simple matter – track him down, take him back."

"It's more complicated than that."

"How?"

"Here's the thing, Jon."

"What?"

"You might know him."

Reznick felt his stomach knot. "You mind explaining?"

Meyerstein opened her briefcase and passed him a black-and-white photo.

Reznick stared at it. He recognized the man in the picture. Slightly puffier than he remembered.

"You know him, don't you?"

"You know full well I do."

Meyerstein pulled out another photo and passed it over. In color, a bit faded, showing Reznick and the same man in Baghdad. "He's ex-Delta too, isn't he?"

Reznick stared long and hard at the picture.

"He poses a considerable danger to the American public till he's caught."

"And he heads up a militia?"

"Amongst other things."

"Like what?"

"Numerous analysts are working on this as we speak."

"You wanna cut the shit, Meyerstein? What's he planning? What do you know?"

"Timothy McVeigh ... ring a bell?"

"Course. Oklahoma bomber. Blew up the Federal Building, right?"

"Cain worshipped him. Had a picture up on his cell wall."

Reznick looked out of the window and shook his head. "Fuck."

"Bottom line? This former Delta operator's planning to carry out a terrorist attack. Large-scale."

"Got any details?"

"Analysis shows it'll be here on American soil, against American citizens. And before you ask, that's all we know."

THREE

Hunter Cain saw the farmhouse lights up ahead; no power lines for miles. He pressed on down the dirt road as the headlights lit up his path. Ahead he saw the owner, silhouetted on his front porch, carrying a shotgun and flashlight. The old man used the beam of the light to guide Cain to a huge open barn.

Cain drove inside and pulled up beside a 50s Buick. He switched off the ignition and slid the keys under the seat. Then he got out, hauled a tarpaulin over his car and headed into the house.

The old man patted him on the back. "You'll be safe here."

Cain nodded. "Need a shower and a fresh set of clothes."

"All in your room. Anything else?"

"You gotta burn my clothes."

"No problem. Leave them in the basket outside your room."

"What time you up?"

"Four."

"You wanna wake me then?"

"Okay."

Cain hugged the old man tight. He felt strangely elated. "Great to breathe fresh air again."

"No one'll catch you here, I promise."

Cain went upstairs, showered and got into his bed. His mind raced as he stared up at the ceiling fan, his thoughts making sleep impossible.

At 4.03 the old man shook Cain from his sleep. He put on khaki tee shirt, combat trousers, black boots, and headed downstairs. A radio played classical music softly in the background.

The old man served him a bowl of porridge, scrambled eggs and toast, freshly squeezed orange juice and coffee. They sat silently. No need for small talk.

The old man left the table and returned a few minutes later with a backpack.

"What've we got here?" Cain asked.

"New ID papers, fake passport, and ten thousand dollars in cash for living costs."

Cain nodded. Smart. No credit cards. "What else?"

"Just what I was told to get you. Two 9mm Glocks, foldaway sniper rifle, knives, ammo, maps, layout. It's all there."

"Good man."

When the first shards of sunlight peeked over the horizon, the old man drove Cain nearly a mile down a back road to a clearing in the woods. It was a makeshift shooting range. The targets were life-size mannequins. More than two hundred yards away. He pulled the rifle from the backpack confidently. Had it locked and loaded in seconds.

Cain shot each and every target. It didn't take long for him to get his range again. The old man watched, silent again, face impassive. He saw Cain shoot the plastic heads to pieces and leave the mannequins headless. He hadn't shot a gun in years. But his training all those years ago kicked in. It was like he hadn't been away.

The old man drove Cain back to the house and showed him to a basement gym. He worked out for two solid hours. Lifting weights, skipping, using the punching bag, doing hundreds of press-ups and sit-ups till he was bathed in sweat.

He went outside. The old man handed him a bottle of chilled water.

Cain gulped it down and sat on the porch.

"You might want to get some sleep for the rest of the day."

"Why's that?"

"You're on the move once it gets dark."

"Pensacola?"

"Nope."

"Where?"

"Ormond Beach."

"Why the change?"

"We want to do this right. They think Pensacola's … too close to home."

Cain nodded. He saw the logic. "Who's taking me?"

"Me."

"Rendezvous times all in hand?"

"All set. Rest up. We leave as soon as it gets dark."

FOUR

Meyerstein dropped off Jon Reznick on the fifth floor of the FBI's DC HQ and headed up to the seventh floor. Just like the fifth, but highly secure. She could see the cameras watching him. The door said "Director." She knocked twice, not too loud.

"It's open."

Meyerstein walked in and he pointed to a seat the other side of his desk.

"You look terrible. You okay?"

Meyerstein sat down and shifted in her seat. She couldn't abide small talk about how people look, especially her. "Why wouldn't I be?"

O'Donoghue sighed and steepled his fingers. "Martha, I'm sorry I have to raise this again, but we have a problem."

"I'm well aware of that, sir. Joint terrorism team already assembled."

"I mean Jon Reznick."

Meyerstein said nothing.

"What is it with you and him?"

Meyerstein felt herself flush. "I beg your pardon, sir?"

"This will be the fourth time you've included him in a major investigation. And, yes, while the results speak for themselves, there are murmurings."

"What kind of murmurings?"

"They say he's getting into the heart of the FBI, and they don't know anything about him. They feel uneasy. Is he linked to the CIA? That's all they want to know."

"And who exactly is *they*, sir?"

O'Donoghue picked up a piece of paper from his desk. He paused with it in his hand for a few moments before he handed it to her. "Read."

Meyerstein saw the Department of Homeland Security seal. A personal letter from the director, dated six weeks earlier, outlining his "continuing concerns" over the legality and ethics of deploying Reznick in an "unspecified role" within "highly sensitive FBI investigations." Her stomach tightened. He wanted Reznick out and Meyerstein "relieved of her duties." She felt her heart rate quicken. "And you've been sitting on this for six weeks?"

O'Donoghue said nothing.

Meyerstein took a few moments to compose herself. She thought of her senior position within the FBI. And how she'd worked herself to the bone for years, pursuing investigations. She knew her health was suffering. She wondered, yet again, if it was all worth it. "Sir, do you think I do a good job?"

O'Donoghue sighed. "I think you do a great job."

"So?"

"So … Look, Martha, sometimes it all comes down to politics."

"Sir, I don't give a damn about politics, internal struggles within an organization, all that bullshit. I'm committed to my family, like we all are. But I'm focussed on the work. Keeping our country safe. I won't let anything get in the way of that."

"Martha, doing nothing is not an option. Homeland Security needs this issue addressed."

"And what exactly do you propose?"

"I want you to do your job, but without Reznick on the team."

"Listen to me, sir. On this particular case, more than ever, I believe Jon Reznick is the perfect fit for my team. He knows Hunter Cain."

"How?"

"Delta."

O'Donoghue sighed long and hard. He looked at Meyerstein with a withering gaze.

"What?"

"Martha, there are murmurings within the FBI about Reznick's role. It's bothering people. There's talk about your relationship with him."

"What the hell does that mean?"

"Hang on – people think you and him might be an item. Heart ruling head. They say it's unprofessional."

"Now listen here, my relationship with Jon Reznick is strictly professional. Strictly."

"Your personal life, family, all that, of course it's

your private concern. But when it crosses over into work, no one likes it."

"Do you think I'm having some sort of relationship with him?"

O'Donoghue shifted in his seat.

"Is that it?" She raised her eyebrows.

"I don't know."

"It's true he's been part of my most pivotal investigations, but each and every time he's been inscrutable. His instincts, his critical thinking ... phenomenal."

"Do you like him?"

"What does that mean?"

"Do you like him?"

"Yes, I like him. A lot. But I also admire him."

"I believe he lost his wife in 9/11."

Meyerstein felt her throat tighten. "Yes, that's right."

"Have you ever seen the CIA file on Reznick?"

"No."

"Makes interesting reading."

"How so?"

"Martha, this guy is ... he's out there."

"You want to explain how he's *out there*?"

"There was an investigation after an incident in Iraq. His unit was training members of the Iraqi army, and some Ba'athist sleeper opened fire on two of his Delta colleagues."

"I didn't know that."

"There's more."

Meyerstein shrugged.

"Reznick killed the guy with one headshot."

"I would expect nothing less."

"The Afghan had already been overpowered and he was in handcuffs. It's a war crime."

Meyerstein said nothing.

"The Afghan had a brother. Reznick put a gun to his head till he was told who gave the orders."

"Jon Reznick is an honorable soldier and a fine man."

"Putting a gun to a defenseless man's head is not what we're about."

"Sometimes we need people like Jon Reznick. I wasn't there. Neither were you. We don't know what it was like."

"Martha, okay, here's what I'm going to do. I hear what you're saying. And I get that. But I need a commitment from you that this issue will be addressed as a matter of urgency."

"I can give that, but not just now. I have work to do."

"I'm going to write to Homeland Security and suggest you head across there to speak with them direct. How does that sound? It's the best I can do."

"Fine."

Meyerstein got to her feet. "Anything else, sir?"

"Be careful. And keep an eye on Reznick."

Meyerstein said nothing.

"I don't like the sound of this case. Red flags all over the place."

FIVE

Reznick took some more coffee as he sat around an oval table on the fifth floor of the FBI's Washington headquarters along with the rest of Meyerstein's hand-picked team. He'd been introduced to a plethora of counter-terrorism specialists from US intelligence agencies. CIA, Homeland Security, NSA. Plus federal police and a US marshal. And FBI profiler and behavioral analyst Michael Malone.

When Meyerstein walked in and sat down, she arranged a pile of papers, briefing documents and her iPad in front of her. There was a huge screen on the wall. She picked up a remote control and pointed it at the screen. It flashed up a picture of Cain taken inside Leavenworth US Penitentiary, Kansas. The eyes hooded. Cold, dead blue.

Reznick stared long and hard at the picture as the memories flooded back.

"People don't usually escape from Leavenworth," Meyerstein said. "I know it, you know it, and I'm sure most of the prison population of America knows it. But this man, Hunter Cain, managed that feat. Quite something. Quite, quite something."

A few nods as others scribbled down notes.

Reznick had showered in her office beforehand and freshened up with a new set of clothes. He gulped some more black coffee as his system was roused from the previous night's booze. He'd also popped a Dexedrine, which did the trick. His senses were finally switching on.

Meyerstein stared at the screen. "What do we know about this guy? Caucasian male, forty-one years old, spent nearly a decade inside after being given a twenty-year stretch for terrorism offences. He was raised in Florida, but we can't assume he'll return there. He's highly dangerous. Propensity for extreme violence."

A man in a gray suit cleared his throat. "Assistant Director, James Harrison, Central Intelligence Agency. I think it is important at the outset that I put my cards on the table."

Meyerstein shrugged. "Sure."

"We have a record of Hunter Cain working overseas briefly as a security contractor in Baghdad."

"For?"

"Gemini Solutions. Based out of Atlanta."

"We haven't got that. Why hasn't that been passed on?"

Harrison shifted in his seat. "It's the Agency. You know how it is."

"No, I don't know how it is, James. What the hell is the point if we don't share information?"

"There's a feeling that if we have an asset ..."

Meyerstein stared at him. "I'm sorry, an asset? You're saying Cain is one of your guys?"

Harrison leaned back in his seat. He looked uneasy. "He was known to us. He was a point of contact within that firm."

"Point of contact?"

"He was passing on intelligence."

"Go on."

"He worked alongside Shia paramilitaries at one time; we wanted to know what was happening. His crew tagged along with them in the early days of the liberation, but gradually he started feeding us information on these guys. Where they were based. Their alliances. Where they hung out. And from there, we got an entry into Shia politicians. We were able to work with them, identifying Ba'athists, you know the stuff."

"When did Cain leave Gemini?"

"Late 2006."

"Then he went home?"

"Pretty poor mental state. Some described him as clean gone."

"Did he get help?"

"He dropped off our radar."

"I see. And then ..."

"And then, he apparently formed this militia."

"Did you know about them? Did you try and make contact with him?"

"I don't know what happened."

Meyerstein folded her arms. "So we've got this

disturbed, highly trained killing machine who's been brutalized in Iraq?"

Harrison nodded.

Meyerstein's gaze wandered round the table. "Jon Reznick, who some of you will already know, was in Delta Force. He actually knows Cain from their time together." She looked across at Reznick. "First, we need to track him down. But assuming we do, give me some more about this guy."

Reznick leaned back in his seat, all eyes on him. "Hunter Cain, like all Delta operators, is very self-contained. He can happily work alone, or in a team. Phenomenally fit, as you'd expect. But what set him apart was his intelligence. High critical-thinking skills. Comfortable with high-pressure situations, again like all Delta. Most interesting facet? Sadist. Enjoyed killing. So much so that he once cut off the fingers of a Taliban prisoner as a keepsake. Big one for trophies."

Meyerstein asked, "Political ideology?"

"Far right from day one. A lot of Delta are what you'd describe as military right-wing – protecting the homeland and swearing allegiance to the flag are givens. But he was something quite, quite different."

"Fascist tendencies perhaps?"

"Borderline. He read Nietzsche, books on philosophy, Goethe, and Adolf Hitler. Whole passages he could recite verbatim. Geo-political buff."

Malone was scribbling notes furiously. "You mind if I jump in here, Jon?"

Reznick shrugged.

"I've worked with Jon and the Assistant Director before. So from what Jon says, this is a highly intelligent man. This is an interesting challenge in front of us, for sure. I've been reading up on Hunter Cain. Propensity to extreme violence from an early age. Father whipped him if he didn't finish his meals. So we can have a clear insight into his psychological make-up. Certified sane apparently, but examples of him hearing voices as a child. Perhaps may hint at schizophrenia. But this has never been diagnosed."

Reznick blew out his cheeks. "Are you saying he could've been in Delta, and subjected to everything we had to go through, and be schizophrenic? Is that possible?"

"Far more likely to be psychopathic, perhaps." He stared long and hard at Reznick. "But to answer your question: yes, I believe it would be possible. Could he be delusional?"

Reznick said nothing.

"There could be multiple personalities at work here, to be frank. The cutting off of fingers, or any body part, is part of the make-up of many serial killers."

Meyerstein stared at her notes before she fixed her gaze on Reznick. She then looked across at her FBI colleague. "Militia guy, military training, tough, possible personality disorder, hatred of government, fixation with Timothy McVeigh, on the loose.

I've not had time to look over what the prison says, but where are we with that?"

Female Special Agent Gillian Miller cleared her throat. "It's clear this was pre-planned, months in advance. Clearly having expert help on the outside, almost certainly on the inside too. Governor has suspended one officer he suspects of being intimidated by associates of Cain to ignore shanks in his cell, made from scrap metal, which we believe were used to cut away at the seal round the toilet before it was ripped out."

"What about the plans for the building? Who has access to these?"

"Just about anyone. Not difficult to find. I accessed encrypted plans online couple of hours ago. Militia groups exchange intelligence all the time, always highly encrypted."

Meyerstein shook her head. "Jon, capabilities for a guy like this? I'm not looking for referenced articles, obviously; just your take on what this could mean."

"I think you got a serious problem. This is not, as your colleague Special Agent Miller said, just a guy that got lucky. We're talking maximum security. People don't just walk out of places like that unless there's a highly technical network in place. I'm talking planning, strategy for execution, and it would take time. And they couldn't get it wrong, as he'd be on 24/7 solitary, with no chance of escape. There's clearly a target on the outside they've identified.

This guy doesn't like government. But there will no doubt be other stuff he doesn't like. He doesn't like business either. Especially big business. Corporate America he has a major problem with. Small government is his thing. But as for targets, take your pick. Too numerous to mention. Nato summits, G8, anything like that coming up?"

Meyerstein shook her head. "Got a Nato summit in Milan in a week."

Reznick shrugged. "So are we talking about a government target in America? McVeigh's terrorism was clearly a signal from the far-right militia groups of what they thought of federal government control. They don't like control. They don't like government."

Meyerstein stared down at her papers for a few moments as a red light began to flash on her BlackBerry. "Cain and his inner circle are based in the Florida Panhandle. The Panhandle. That's where his contacts are. That's where he has family and friends."

Special Agent Miller piped up, "We have no evidence he's there or headed there."

"But in the circumstances, you have to start with what you know. We know to focus on Florida. And we need to assume he's either getting help from Florida or headed directly there."

Reznick cleared his throat. "What concerns me is: who's behind Cain? His backers. He's not doing this alone. Any ideas?"

Meyerstein spoke. "The militias are all pretty self-contained, divided into cells. But there's a degree of cross-fertilization of ideas and people."

"But we need to find out who's backing this, or else we're gonna be chasing shadows."

Meyerstein sighed. "Do you think this is imminent?"

"Highly likely. The shorter Cain is on the outside, the smaller the chance of him getting caught."

"Can you be more specific?"

"Think seventy-two hours max."

SIX

The pick-up truck pulled up outside the windowless biker clubhouse bar outside Ormond Beach. Hunter Cain pulled his baseball cap down low as he watched a guy sitting astride a chopper. The biker turned and nodded in their direction.

The driver said, "That's him. Solid."

"Where's he from?"

"Outlaws chapter in Oakland, California. Originally. Runs a small garage not far from here."

Cain said nothing.

The guy on the bike pulled out a cellphone. He nodded and glanced across in the direction of the pick-up. He ended the call and put the phone in his jacket pocket. Then he signaled.

The driver said, "That's your cue, Hunter. Best of luck."

Cain leaned over and hugged the driver tight. "I won't need luck. They'll be the ones needing luck."

The driver said, "They'll be in touch."

Cain got out of the truck and headed past the

biker and into the bar. The place was empty. He sat down on a stool and looked at the barman. "Gimme a Heineken, son."

The barman nodded nervously and handed over a chilled Heineken.

Cain gulped down the cold beer. It felt phenomenal. His first for years.

The barman wiped the wooden counter. "You on vacation my friend?"

"No."

The barman nodded slowly. He stared at the tattoos on Cain's neck. "You just outta the joint."

"You ask a lot of questions. Gimme another beer."

The barman served him up another chilled Heineken. "I didn't mean any disrespect. Just I got out last year myself. Four fuckin' years, man."

Cain said nothing as he chugged back the second beer. He turned and looked around the rest of the room, walls adorned with pictures of bikers and their girls partying in the bar.

The clubhouse door opened and in walked two tattooed white guys. He recognized them immediately. They walked up to Cain and hugged him tight, then sat down either side of him at the bar.

The guy to his left smiled. "You all set?"

Cain nodded.

The barman handed the scar-faced guy a Heineken.

"Hey, Pete," Cain greeted him.

"I'm in charge of getting you safely to your destination," Pete replied.

Cain looked at the barman. "And what about this guy? Is he with you guys?"

Without a word, the newcomer took out a handgun and shot the barman at point-blank range through the head. The sound echoed round the wooden bar, blood exploded, and the man's body slumped to the floor.

Cain's ears were ringing. "I'll take that as a no."

Pete holstered his gun and hugged Cain tight. "Good to see you again, Hunter. How the fuck are you?"

"Same old, same old."

The guy on the left got off his stool and hugged Cain. "I'm gonna do whatever it takes, Hunter. You know me."

"Neil, nice to see you, bro."

Cain grinned. It felt good to see two of his crew again, both released six months earlier. "We got work to do. But first, you need to dispose of that guy's body."

Neil hopped over the counter and opened the hatch on the floor. Dragging the body feet-first, he dropped it down into the cellar and slammed the hatch shut. "All done."

Cain looked at Pete. "Who was the kid behind the bar?"

"Friend of the Outlaws. Worthless piece of shit. Skag-head. Better off dead."

Cain said, "So we all set?"

Pete nodded. "We got a fresh set of wheels waiting outside."

They drove for over an hour south down I-95 and stopped off at a gas station. They switched to a waiting SUV. Cain got in the passenger seat as the other two got in the rear.

The driver gave him a firm handshake. "Let's get going."

Cain nodded as they drove inland into the heart of Florida. Past little towns, villages and into open space. Farmland. Down some dirt tracks.

At last they pulled up at a rural farmhouse.

The driver said, "He's waiting."

Cain turned to face Pete and Neil. His two comrades. "I'll see you soon. We're gonna kick some ass, right?"

Both nodded, stone-faced.

Cain pushed open the door and headed inside, alone. Standing at the far end of the hall was a huge man wearing a camouflage jumpsuit, hunting rifle in one hand. He stepped forward and hugged him tight.

"Good to have you here, Hunter."

"Let's get started."

"Follow me."

Cain followed the man down into a basement cellar. There was a huge plan on the wall.

"This is the layout of the building where

they're meeting," he said. "Specifications, dimensions, access routes, stairwells, everything. Copy of the original plans. No modifications since it was built."

Cain stepped forward and stared at the plans. "Who knows about this?"

"A handful of people. Good people. Us."

"Pete and Neil?"

"Where they're going, they'll have access to this plan too. Five copies made."

Cain had never met the man. He had only heard of him in militia circles. His accent sounded Appalachian. He'd served with a few in Delta. Tough diehards.

"You're probably wondering why we picked you, right?"

"It had crossed my mind."

"We needed someone who was top-grade military. We needed someone with our mindset. A freeman. But someone who wasn't averse to doing what it took to reclaim our country."

Cain looked at the map for a few moments. "What else?"

"We picked your friends because we'd been observing how tight you lot were inside Leavenworth."

"You got people inside?"

"We have eyes and ears everywhere."

"But why particularly me?"

"A good few of the Aryan Brotherhood were

excellent candidates. We wanted someone who was as tough as those fucks, but stood apart."

"Well, by now they'll know I'm out. And I'll be on their wanted list."

"Let us deal with that."

The guy bent over and opened up a floor hatch. Cain peered down and saw a ladder into a well-lit tunnel. "Go on."

Cain climbed down and the man followed after.

The man was panting heavily as they entered a brightly-lit air-conditioned tunnel. "Follow me."

Cain did as he was told. "What the fuck is this?"

"You'll see."

They walked for nearly a mile till they got to a huge, floodlit firing range.

"State of the art. Hidden from view. Soundproofed. Emergency exits in four places, in case the house is raided."

Cain smiled. He realized the mission was in good hands.

SEVEN

It was late when the small plane carrying Reznick, Meyerstein and a dozen Feds touched in Pensacola. He wondered how things would unfold. He always liked to think ahead. They were driven to the FBI field office and briefed by local members of the joint terrorism task force, specializing in organized crime and penitentiary gangs.

Reznick pulled up a seat and listened intently. He realized that anything with Cain involved would be serious stuff. Heavy-duty. A huge color photo of Cain was projected on to a wall as they sat around an oval table, drinking coffee and eating pizza slices.

"We believe," began Special Agent Cortez of Pensacola FBI field office, "that Cain moved south. NSA have been called in and have pinpointed GPS locations with voice analysis from a cellphone microphone. In particular, to the wife of a militia member in Louisiana, Edwin Mackenzie. He was previously a member of a neo-Nazi biker gang, Kavallerie Brigade. He hasn't been seen for a couple of days, around the same time Cain went missing.

We believe Mackenzie was instrumental in getting him from Kansas down south and handed over, almost certainly to another militia."

Reznick said, "Anything else on this Mackenzie?"

"Periphery of the Aryan Brotherhood around twenty years ago in Leavenworth. Killed two prison guards with a homemade shank. He escaped alongside Cain. But a subsequent search of his cell revealed notes written in invisible ink. Code numbers that we believe were the time and date of the escape."

Reznick rubbed his eyes. "Great."

Cortez said, "We believe now that Mackenzie was the bridge between Kansas and Florida, where Cain knows a lot of people. Pensacola in particular."

"He won't be heading to Pensacola," interjected Reznick.

Cortez looked around the table at the rest of the FBI agents as Meyerstein scribbled notes. "I'm sorry. I don't think I've been introduced. You are?"

Meyerstein interrupted. "His name is Jon Reznick. He works on special projects for me. Got a problem with that, Special Agent Cortez?"

"Absolutely not, ma'am – just looking for clarification."

"Well, you've got it." Meyerstein looked across at Reznick. "So, Jon, would you like to clarify why you think he won't be heading to Pensacola?"

Reznick sighed. "Here's the thing. He might know people round here, but he isn't stupid. He's very intelligent. I know this guy. If he's in Florida, he won't be hanging around Pensacola."

Cortez said, "Are you saying we just shouldn't bother about intel we have on him and his militia buddies?"

"Not at all. What I'm saying is, you won't find Hunter Cain here. He'll be on the move. Hidden from sight by now. But not here."

"Mr Reznick ..."

"Listen, Cortez, I'm sure you're very good at your job putting a solid investigative case together. But you need to get down to a different level if you're dealing with these guys."

Cortez looked at Meyerstein before staring across at Reznick. "Are you saying we break the law?"

"I say the speed you guys work on investigations is irrelevant to finding Hunter Cain. He's been sprung from a high-security penitentiary. And most of us in this room think something's afoot. A terrorist act, maybe – who knows? And lives will be lost."

"Reznick, we need to do things in a legal, cogent manner. We need to cover all bases."

"And, meanwhile, he's out there getting further away."

Meyerstein cleared her throat. "What are you suggesting, Jon?"

"I'm suggesting we need to work this investigation from a different angle. Find out where his acquaintances hang out, and go in for a little chat."

Cortez grinned and shook his head. "Just like that."

Reznick took a few moments to compose himself. He wanted to go across and smash Cortez in the jaw. "Would you feel uncomfortable doing that?"

Meyerstein lifted her hand to silence the exchange. "Oh, that's enough. Special Agent Cortez, it's a fair point Jon raises."

"Is it, ma'am?"

Meyerstein slammed her hand hard down on the table. "Who the hell do you think you're talking to?"

Cortez flushed crimson. "Ma'am?"

"Don't ever try and play the smartass with me. If you're asked a question, don't be so goddamn defensive and precious. Now, let's try again and get an answer. Where do the acquaintances of Hunter Cain hang out? Who's the top one? And I'm looking for one with connections to the Kavallerie Brigade, and any militia activity."

Cortez nodded. He switched on a laptop. They watched a collection of photos appear on the screen. Bikers knocking back drinks, playing pool, and even one having sex with a girl on the pool table. "There's a clubhouse, owned by the Outlaws biker gang, just outside Pensacola. Cain knows quite a few of the guys in there. Bought and sold guns with them. And drugs. Felony violations go on all the time. Was shut down. Burned down at one time. But rebuilt within days and opened up with a new owner on the license."

Reznick stared long and hard at the pictures. "Nice crowd."

Cortez said, "If we're going to go in there we need to prepare, and have extensive back-up. It'll take days to get things in place. We can't just go in hard."

"Why not?" Reznick asked.

"Why not? Because I know from experience that any criminal activity has to be monitored, and then arrests made. Unless we know Cain is on the premises, we're on thin ice if we want prosecutions."

Reznick said, "Who said anything about prosecutions?"

Cortez shrugged. "I'm sorry. I don't follow."

Reznick said, "Do you have reasonable belief that there's drug dealing going on there?"

"Yeah, I believe that's the case. But that's a world away from going in there and making arrests, and getting some speed- or methamphetamine-heads."

"Who said anything about making arrests?"

"I'm sorry, Mr Reznick, I really don't follow."

Reznick looked around the table and fixed his gaze on Meyerstein. "You know as well as I do, time is against us. We also don't know shit where Cain's gone. But we sure as hell won't find him by twiddling our thumbs. I say we go to that bar and ask around."

Cortez shook his head and bit his lower lip as if trying to stifle a laugh. "Mr Reznick, and what do you think they'll say?"

"It depends how you ask the question. We need to go in there, get control, and exert some pressure on them."

Cortez stared at him long and hard. "With all due respect, I don't think you know what you're talking about."

"Special Agent Cortez, with all due respect, I don't give a flying fuck what you think. And I don't care for your rules, regulations and all your other bullshit you claim you need."

"We operate under the law, Reznick."

"You must be very naïve or very dumb, Cortez. Sometimes, just sometimes, you need to play dirty. Do you understand what I'm saying?"

Cortez said nothing.

Meyerstein cleared her throat. "Jon, that's quite enough. It's true our leads are all tied to who he knew in and around Pensacola. But barging in like Special Agent Cortez says without thinking of the downside would be pointless."

"Here's the thing," Reznick continued. "You have nothing just now, right?"

Meyerstein nodded.

"Now, I know Hunter, and he's not stupid. He won't be at one of his old haunts, or a friend's house. I'll guarantee that. But what you can do is get inside his head. And maybe, just maybe, he'll make a mistake."

Cortez shrugged. "And how exactly are we going to get inside his head?"

"You'll see." Reznick stared at Meyerstein. "We have nothing to lose. There's no downside."

"You want to go into that clubhouse, don't you? And then what?"

Reznick shrugged. "Ask a few questions, that's all."

It was dark when the three SUVs headed down an unlit road. Palm trees fringed the sand dunes. Reznick sat up front; three plainclothes Feds took the back. Four each in the other two vehicles. But Meyerstein opted to stay back at base and watch things unfold in real time on the pinhole cameras attached to tee shirts, lapels and jackets.

Reznick felt wired. He saw the lights of the clubhouse come into view. Rock music getting louder in the steambath air. He turned to the guys in the back seat. "Okay, you guys, you're coming in with me. As agreed, we keep the other two cars outside for back-up."

The Feds nodded, faces impassive.

"I walk in first, okay? You give me ten seconds. And then you come in."

More nods.

Reznick opened the door. The sound of a deep bass and guitar riffs filled the sticky air. Laughing. Shouting. He got out of the car and strode up to the door. Stared through the tiny hatch. Around a dozen boozed-up bikers, a few girls danced for them, guzzling Jack Daniel's whiskey and beer.

He pushed open the door and walked towards the clear leader, a sneering fuck, legs wide, a girl grinding before him.

A long-hair pulled up a pool cue in front of him and Reznick grabbed it off him. He smashed the guy hard in the jaw, blood pouring down his split temple.

A few bikers approached him.

Reznick knocked the first out cold. He rabbit-punched the second and kicked the third in the balls. They dropped to the floor, writhing.

He pushed his way past the girl.

The biker with his legs astride stared at him, eyes cold.

Reznick took out his 9mm and shoved it in the biker's gaping mouth. "Okay, I got a few questions."

The guy's eyes were wide with terror.

Reznick heard the door burst open and the Feds stormed in. Shotguns and handguns.

"Everyone on the floor!" one Fed shouted.

A biker a couple of feet away began to laugh. "Fuck you!"

Reznick pulled the 9mm from the biker's mouth and shot the other biker in the stomach. The noise exploded round the bar. The shot biker shrieked in pain as blood poured from his belly. "I said everyone on the fucking floor!"

Everyone complied as the guy on the floor began to cry.

Reznick pushed the gun back into the biker's mouth.

The man's eyes were crazed.

"Okay, you can see how this thing works. Now, simple question. I'm looking for someone who knows Hunter Cain."

The man shook his head.

Reznick pressed the gun to the back of the biker's mouth. "If you don't give me the correct answer, you're gonna die. So I'm gonna count back from three, got it? Here goes. Three ... two ..."

"Wait!" the guy spluttered. "Wait the fuck!"

Reznick took the gun from his mouth and pressed it to his forehead. "Yeah?"

"Man, the thing is, I know Hunter, but I don't wanna ..."

A woman's voice piped up from the throng. "I know Hunter Cain."

Reznick spun around and saw a scantily clad young woman face down on the floor. He kept the gun trained on the biker. "How?"

"I'm his girlfriend. I see him once a month."

Reznick pointed at her. "Get yourself outside, go to the last car and wait for me."

The girl got to her feet and headed outside.

Reznick pressed the gun tight against the biker's head. He watched as pee began to dribble onto the floor through the guy's jeans. "Think you need to change your pants, son."

He turned and walked out as the Feds with shotguns and handguns covered him.

Reznick walked over to the last vehicle and saw

that the biker chick was sitting in the back. He climbed in beside her. He waited till the Feds had left the bar, got back in their SUV and pulled away. They followed behind, leaving a trail of dust in their wake as they about-turned down the beach road and back to Pensacola.

The girl said, "Who the hell are you? You're not a Fed, are you?"

Reznick said, "They are. I'm working alongside them on this case. We're looking for Hunter Cain. How long've you been his girlfriend?"

"Since forever."

"I heard he was married."

"Still is. I'm his … girlfriend."

"I see."

Reznick handed her Meyerstein's card. She looked at it long and hard.

"Okay, so this is an FBI business card, right?" she said.

"We need to speak to Hunter urgently."

The girl began to sob. "Fuck!"

"Tell me, you got any kids?"

"Three. Two from my ex-husband, who was a dog, let me tell you."

"And the third?"

"That's Hunter's."

"We don't have a record of that."

"He took my name. Hunter isn't on any certificate or whatever."

"What's your name?"

The girl pushed some hair away from her eyes, tears streaking her face with mascara. "Kathleen. Kathleen Burke."

"Kathleen, I'm glad you were smart enough to speak up. But it's really important Hunter contacts us. Now you seem like a nice enough girl. But, to be honest, you really don't wanna hang around with that crowd back there. You got a record?"

"A few for drugs. One coming up soon."

"We might be able to help you with that. But for that, we need to speak to Hunter."

The girl dabbed her eyes.

"You need to pass on a message if he calls."

"And what's that?"

"Tell Hunter that Jon Reznick is wanting to speak to him. I know Hunter pretty good. We were in Delta together, way back."

The girl nodded.

"Jon Reznick. You want me to write that down?"

The girl nodded.

Reznick scribbled down his name and handed the card back to her. "That's got my name on it, and this lady's number. Hunter can contact me direct on her cellphone."

"What if he doesn't call me?"

"Let me worry about that."

EIGHT

Meyerstein was in a conference room in the FBI's Pensacola field office, watching a rerun of the footage on one of the big screens, coffee in hand, as her second in command, Special Agent Roy Stamper, paced the floor. "You wanna sit down, Roy?"

Stamper shook his head. "I warned you about this sort of thing, Martha. I warned time and time again. This is what happens when we allow crazies like Reznick in on our work."

Meyerstein said nothing. She felt uneasy about the methods Reznick had used, and couldn't see any upside. The illegality was clear.

"Threatening to kill a biker in a clubhouse? That's outrageous. Illegal. And, frankly, the stuff of nightmares. If this gets out, and mark my words it will, we're fucked. We'll be crucified."

"Quiet!"

"No I won't! I've put up with this sort of bullshit for too long, Martha. What in God's name is the director going to say about this?"

Meyerstein ran a hand through her hair. "It's not ideal, I see that."

"Not ideal? Are you kidding me? It's outrageous. It's illegal. Immoral. It's frankly embarrassing that this behavior was carried out in the name of the FBI. Never in my wildest dreams would I have imagined us doing that."

Meyerstein stared at the footage, seething. "I said, enough!"

"That's a law suit waiting to happen. It's just a matter of time."

"I'll deal with it."

"But you know what gets me, Martha? The lack of purpose. There's no point to it. There's no gain."

Meyerstein switched off the footage with a remote control and stared at Stamper. "Roy, tell me, have your guys come up with any concrete leads so far?"

He sighed. "No, we haven't. But we sure as hell didn't ram guns into people's mouths. Martha, chrissakes, this isn't Iraq. This is America. I'm at a loss to understand why you tolerate this guy."

"The reason I tolerate him, as you describe it, is that on each and every investigation he's been with me, he's not only delivered, he's saved lives."

"And this time?"

"I'll talk to him about this. I agree, it's unacceptable."

"Unacceptable? Unacceptable? It's the actions of a burnt-out crazy."

Meyerstein sat down and leaned back in a leather seat, hands behind her head. A silence opened up between them. Only the low growl of the air-conditioning unit and the hum of the computers disturbed the quiet.

A knock at the door, and a young rookie agent popped his head round. "Ma'am, they'll be back in two minutes."

Meyerstein nodded, staring at the ceiling.

The young agent shut the door.

Meyerstein said, "Roy, can you leave me with my thoughts just now?"

Stamper stared at her long and hard. "Of course."

"Send in Jon Reznick when he gets back."

"What about the rest of the team for the debrief?"

"Just Reznick."

Stamper left the conference room. A couple of minutes later Reznick walked in.

"You looking for a debrief?"

"Shut the door behind you."

Reznick shut the door quietly behind him. He pulled up a seat and slumped down. "You're not very good at concealing your feelings, Meyerstein. What is it?"

Meyerstein leaned forward. "What is it? Let me think. Is it the forcing a gun into a guy's mouth, the shooting, the countless violations of the Constitution, breaking our US laws, and God knows what else?"

Reznick said nothing.

"What the hell were you thinking?"

Reznick blew out his cheeks.

"I'm waiting for an answer. I'm very close to taking you off this team, Jon. I don't want to. But this is absolutely not what we're about."

"Oh yeah, and what are you about? Waiting to get a goddamn lead that might never turn up? Listen, sometimes, you just have to push back and sometimes people get hurt. Egos get bruised."

"This is not about egos getting bruised. It's about a man getting shot."

"A man? Every one of those fuckers in there is a felon. You know it, I know it, and every goddamn other person knows it."

"We have rules for a reason."

"Those rules are worthless when you're up against people like Hunter Cain. You need to try and get into their heads, like I said."

"And did it work?"

"I could do without the sarcasm, thanks. Actually, did it work? We'll just have to wait and see."

A knock at the door.

"Come in!" Meyerstein said.

The door opened and Stamper walked in. "Martha, can I have a word?"

"What is it?"

"Update from the hospital. The shot biker has lost consciousness. And the one who got smashed with the pool cue has bleeding on the brain. They're about to operate."

Meyerstein stared at the floor and sighed. "Keep

me informed if there are any developments, Roy. That'll be all just now."

Stamper shut the door.

Meyerstein took a few moments to compose herself as she looked across at Reznick. "Bleeding on the brain, and another bleeding out in surgery and unconscious. Great, just great."

Reznick said nothing.

"Do you know what I'm going to have to deal with now?"

Reznick shook his head.

"The directors of the FBI and Homeland Security are almost certainly going to be pressing charges against you. And you know what? I couldn't do anything about it. Did you think of that before you stormed in there?"

"We've had this kind of discussion before."

"This time you've crossed the line."

"Sometimes, you need to ruffle the feathers. You need to get in close. They've got to see you, smell you, and see where it takes you."

"I didn't expect you to go in there and act like that."

"Didn't you? What did you expect? Did you expect me just to rock up there, stroll up to the bar and get a Heineken, and start playing pool with them?"

"I expected you to get in and out, armed as you were, without this carnage. What it also means is that the focus is taken away from the hunt for Cain. It's just not okay, Jon."

The conference-room phone rang. "Goddamn." She leaned over and picked up. "Meyerstein! What?"

"Sir, let me get back to you in five minutes. I'm dealing with it."

Meyerstein hung up. "Well, that's just completed the circle. The director of the FBI is wanting me back in DC right away." She put her head in her hands. "Goddamn."

Reznick said nothing.

The minutes dragged as they sat in awkward silence till Meyerstein's cellphone rang.

"Gimme a goddamn break!" She reached into her jacket pocket and pulled out her phone, pressing it to her ear. "Yeah." She frowned. "I'm sorry – who are you?" She handed the phone to Reznick. "It's Kathleen Burke. The girl from the bar. She's crying."

NINE

The SUV with Reznick in the back and Meyerstein in the passenger seat pulled up outside a crummy house in a rundown street on the outskirts of Pensacola. They went inside and upstairs. Kathleen Burke was sitting in her bedroom, drinking a beer, cigarette in hand, tears streaming down her face.

"Okay, you're safe?" Reznick asked.

Burke shook her head.

Reznick went up to her. Her eyes were glazed. "Kathleen, you weren't making much sense. You said your mother called you. And that's all I could make out."

Burke stared blankly at him.

"Your mother? Where's she?"

"She's fine. She looks after my son in Panama City."

"Has he visited her?"

Burke closed her eyes for a moment. "He called her."

"Hunter?"

The girl began to cry. "I'm scared."

Meyerstein punched a number into her cellphone. "What's your mother's number?"

Burke gave it.

"We'll send a specialist team across and get them to a safe house," Meyerstein said. "We need to get your mother and your son out of there. Do you understand?"

Burke nodded. She gave the address and telephone number.

"We'll also do a trace and find where Hunter called from."

Burke said nothing as Meyerstein made the call.

Reznick moved closer to her. "Tell me what happened."

"He's crazy you know. I love him. But he's crazy."

Reznick nodded.

"He warned my mother he would ..."

Burke glanced at Meyerstein and dragged heavily on her cigarette. "You've no fucking idea what he's like."

Reznick said, "I know exactly what he's like, trust me."

"No you don't. You don't know what he's *really* like."

"I know he's a nasty bastard, okay?"

"That doesn't cover the half of it."

"What did he say to your mother, Kathleen?"

Burke slumped to the floor, gulped some beer and crushed her cigarette into an ashtray on a small coffee table. Smoke blew from her nose. "A few years back he raped me. Before he got put away."

Reznick said nothing as Meyerstein headed out into the hall.

"Was this reported?"

"What do you think, I'm crazy?"

"Have these guys got a hold over you?"

"I don't have anyone. Even my mother's more or less disowned me." She rolled up her sleeves and showed the track marks. Scabbed over. "Huh? You think I'm a diabetic? Wrong. I'm a fucking heroin addict. And those guys provide me with whatever they've got. For favors."

Reznick reached out and held her hands between his. "That stops as of now. Do you understand?"

"I can't. He called my mother. He told her he's gonna kill me. He said he's gonna come back and kill me. But first he's gonna rape me. That's what he said. As God is my witness."

"No one's gonna hurt you again, Kathleen. We're gonna get you help. And treatment for your addiction. Whatever it takes. But we need to move you away, for safety."

Burke began to cry, and flung her arms around him. "Don't let him come back. He's fucking crazy."

"You're going to be safe now."

TEN

The sky was burnt orange as the SUV with Hunter Cain and his two militia comrades headed south on I-95. His mind was racing. The message to one of his men in the back seat about Jon Reznick working with the FBI had enraged him. But he wondered if he'd been unduly hasty, contacting Kathleen's mother.

The driver headed off the freeway and pulled up at a diner near Vero Beach. He went in followed by his two comrades.

Cain took a window seat as they tucked into coffee, scrambled eggs, pancakes awash with maple syrup. They ate in silence as country music played loud. The black waitress was bugging him. He leaned close to his two comrades, Pete and Neil. "I need someone in Pensacola taken care of. Today. Who's my best bet that's not on the inside, obviously?"

Neil said, "My brother will do it, if that's what you want. No questions asked."

"I thought he'd moved to Vermont?"

"Came back couple weeks ago."

"Not seen Matt for … ten years, right?"

"Not far off. Who you want dealt with?"

"Kathleen Burke."

Neil said nothing.

"You got a problem with that, Neil?"

"If that's what you want, that's what you'll get."

"I heard Reznick took her out of the bar after shooting up one of the Outlaws, and left another in hospital. They're going to try and turn her against me."

"What's this Reznick like? He a problem for us?"

Cain gulped some of the coffee down. "He's a bad bastard, I know that."

"One of your Delta guys?"

"Absolutely. Never said too much. But he didn't have to."

"Why's that?"

"I fought with him in shitholes across Iraq. Tough as they come."

Neil nodded. "You mentioned Kathleen Burke. Won't they have moved her?"

"They will, most certainly."

"So how will you know where?"

Cain grinned. "Let me worry about that."

"How the hell is that possible? You tracking her cellphone?"

Hunter shook his head and sipped some coffee. "She changes her phone every year, sometimes more."

"So how can you track her?"

"Trust me – I know where she is."

Neil stared at Cain but said nothing.

"I want her taken care of. And I don't care who gets hurt in the process. Do you understand?"

"He'll need to know where she is."

"I'll send that on to him. But I just need you to contact him and ask first if he can do this job."

Neil pulled out his new cellphone, punched in the number for his brother and relayed the message. He nodded. "Whatever it takes, bro." He ended the call.

"We good to go?"

"He says that's not a problem."

"Take the battery and flush it down the toilet."

Neil did that and returned.

Cain smiled and cocked his head, and they followed him back to the SUV, engine running. He climbed into the passenger seat as Neil and Pete got in the back. "Step on it. We got people to kill."

ELEVEN

Reznick was in the bathroom of an FBI safe house on the bayou in an upscale part of Fort Walton Beach, just south of Pensacola. It was a chalet sitting a couple or so miles inland alongside a deepwater boat slip. He splashed cold water on his face. He was relieved they'd gotten Kathleen Burke out of any blowback. She'd been given some methadone, stopping her going cold turkey. He stared at his reflection in the mirror. Dead eyes, pupils like pinpricks after he popped another Dexedrine.

He went upstairs. The living-room blinds were shut as Kathleen Burke chain- smoked cigarettes, filling the room with haze.

Meyerstein said, "Kathleen, if it's okay with you, I'd like to know more about what you and Hunter talked about when you visited."

"Why?"

"We just need to try and build up a picture of him. What he was really like. Leavenworth said he and his crew kept themselves to themselves. Very tight."

"That's true."

"Okay, tell me, your last visit, how did that pan out?"

Burke dragged long on her cigarette, blowing the smoke through the side of her mouth when she exhaled. "He was kinda quiet. We were speaking through glass as we always did, you know, phone to phone."

"Okay, let's talk about what he did say."

Burke looked across at Reznick. "Guy stuff."

Reznick nodded. "He talk politics?"

"Actually, yes he did."

Reznick said, "Was that unusual?"

"Not really."

Reznick turned and looked at Meyerstein. "You okay if I ask a few questions here?"

Meyerstein shook her head. "Go right ahead."

Reznick sat down on the sofa opposite Burke and leaned forward. "I knew Hunter very well in Delta. Now, when you work or play with someone, you get to know things about them. Their moods. Their attitudes. Their views. Getting back to him talking politics, what did he talk about?"

"Jews."

Reznick said nothing as Meyerstein shifted on the sofa.

"He didn't like them. At all. Said one of his guys had killed what he called a Jewish guy in the toilets the previous week."

"What else?"

"The government."

"What about them?"

Burke touched the expensive-looking silver cross round her neck. "He was pretty paranoid. Went on and on about surveillance. Government everywhere. Cursed all the time. When he was finished cursing, he asked about his son."

Reznick nodded.

Meyerstein said, "Kathleen, the clubhouse where you were hanging out … If Hunter wasn't there, what's that all about?"

"Sexual favors in return for some brown, okay?"

"Heroin?"

Reznick stared again at the cross around her neck. He was surprised that a desperate woman like Burke hadn't sold it for drugs.

Burke's eyes filled with tears again. "I'm not proud of what I am. But yes, heroin. Satisfied?"

Meyerstein said, "Did Hunter know about this?"

"Absolutely not."

"What would happen if he did?"

"He'd kill me, and then every goddamn Outlaw he could find. Period. Then he'd burn the place to the ground."

"Kathleen, we're going to get you proper help. This is just the first stage, okay? Your son and mother are safe. And *you* are safe."

"What a mess. What a fucking mess!"

Meyerstein sat down beside her. "Now you're safe here, okay. We'll make sure there are two special agents with you, 24/7, okay?"

Burke nodded, eyes dead.

"Kathleen," Meyerstein said, "before Hunter was jailed, were you living with him? Did he stay overnight, that kind of thing?"

"When he could. He was married." She shrugged. "I know, it's appalling, but I'm not known for making great choices."

"I'm trying to determine more about him. Did any of his friends visit?"

Burke said nothing, a faraway look in her eyes.

Meyerstein grabbed her wrist. "Kathleen, look at me!"

Burke stared at Meyerstein like a frightened rabbit. "Yeah, what?"

"I would expect someone like Hunter to have certain close-knit friends."

Burke nodded.

"Kathleen, you need to help me out here."

"It was a long time ago … eight fucking years."

"What about photos? Have you got any photos?"

Burke shook her head. "He didn't like getting his photograph taken. Really didn't like it one bit."

"Kathleen! Give me some goddamn names! This is some serious shit you're involved with. And you need to give us something in return. Do you understand? We're not messing around."

Burke bit her lower lip and stared at the floor. "There was one characteristic … two guys. But I distinctly remember the same tattoos. Both on the upper arm."

"What kind of tattoos?"

Burke screwed up her face and closed her eyes. "Clovers, you know, shamrocks …"

Meyerstein looked at Reznick and nodded. They both knew what that meant.

"And the initials AB."

Reznick nodded. "Do you know what that means?"

"Aryan Brotherhood. I've heard about them, but Hunter didn't have tattoos like that."

Reznick said nothing.

"They were kinda scary."

"What about names?"

"I can't remember. My memory's not the best."

"And there aren't any photos or mementos?"

"Like I said, Hunter didn't want his photo taken."

Reznick nodded. "Now, this is really important, these two guys, they were regulars, meeting up with Hunter?"

"They were really tight."

"How did you feel when they were around?"

"The Outlaws were just assholes. These guys … they made me feel very scared. When they looked at me, I felt real uneasy."

"Accents?"

"Florida backwoods kind of accent. Maybe Panhandle, but it was definitely down around here."

"What else? Distinguishing features?"

Burke screwed up her face. "The taller of the two had a scar, just above his eye."

"Anything else? What about the other one?"

"Tattoos on his chest too."

Meyerstein said, "Kathleen, we have extensive photographs of Aryan Brotherhood members, both inside and out of jail …"

"I'd recognize them. I can't remember their names. But I'd sure as hell remember what they looked like."

Reznick said, "Kathleen, thinking back all those years ago, was he ever violent to you?"

"He grabbed me by the throat when the mood took him. Tried to throttle me. And before you ask, why did you stay with him, it's because I'm an idiot, an addict, and I'm scared."

Reznick leaned closer. "You're not an idiot. We all make choices in our lives, some better than others. One last thing. I'm trying to think back myself to the Hunter I knew. The guy I knew was aggressive, but focussed. Got the job done. But can you remember if there's a trigger point for him. Something that sets him off."

"He sometimes would wake up in a cold sweat, screaming."

"What was he screaming for?"

"His father. He loved his father."

Meyerstein interrupted. "Our records show his father died when Hunter was a boy."

"His father killed himself. Hunter found him hanging in the loft."

★

Half an hour later, Reznick was in the back of an SUV with Meyerstein, being driven back to the FBI's Pensacola field office, having left a four-man team with Kathleen Burke at the safe house.

Reznick felt wired. He wondered where the whole investigation was going.

Meyerstein pulled out her iPad and opened an attachment to an email from FBI HQ. Two prison mugshots, side by side. She studied the pictures for a few moments before she showed Reznick. "We believe these are the two Aryan Brotherhood nuts she was talking about."

Reznick looked long and hard at the pictures. Hard-core prison inmates. He knew the type. "We sure?"

"As sure as dammit. The guy on the left is Ken 'Mad Dog' Pearce. Certifiable. And on the right is Neil Foley. Aryan Brotherhood's long-term. Incredibly violent. And we believe Hunter Cain's enforcers"

"What else?"

"Just got a message a few moments ago from Stamper's guys. The targets haven't been seen in their homes for the last forty-eight hours."

"Their wives?"

"Not the most cooperative, as you can imagine."

"Okay, so that is something. Two AB wildcards and Hunter. Something must be going down alright."

Meyerstein nodded.

"What about analysis of their plans?"

"We're still working on it. But all analysts are agreed that these two, along with Hunter Cain, are in the early stages of an operation. Almost certainly anti-government terrorism in the McVeigh mold."

Reznick went quiet for a few moments.

"It's a breakthrough of sorts. But I'm still not happy about the methods used to get it."

"Yeah, well …"

"Let's be quite clear, Jon. My job is on the line now. The directors of the FBI and Homeland Security are circling. And I'm damned if I'm going to let them chew me up and spit me out. Do you hear me?"

"I hear you."

"I'm going to let it go this time. But it's the last time."

Reznick stared straight ahead.

"Are we good?"

Reznick turned and smiled. "Damn straight."

Meyerstein's cellphone rang and she groaned. "You're killing me, you do realize that?"

Reznick smiled.

Meyerstein pulled her phone out of her bag. "Roy, what's happening?" She nodded. "Sorry, bad line. On his laptop? Flash stick, okay. Get forensics to look over it and get back to me asap." She nodded. "What kind of letter?" She listened for a few moments. "Get a full analysis." She ended the call.

Reznick said, "Developments?"

"Son of a bitch."

"What is it?"

"Heavily encrypted files on a memory stick at Ken Pearce's house."

"What else?"

"Letter from Hunter Cain to Ken Pearce, congratulating him on the birth of his son, three months ago."

"What's so interesting about that?"

"Ken Pearce has no children. We believe it's a letter using AB code outlining details of the operation."

TWELVE

Meyerstein switched on the huge screen in the conference room at Pensacola FBI as she prepared to videoconference with the directors of the FBI and Homeland Security. She checked the briefings from her team. Hard faces stared down from the split screen. She updated them on the evolving situation.

FBI Director O'Donoghue said, "Martha, the fallout from the Reznick escapade at the biker club-house is spreading. We have threats to Kathleen Burke's mother, who in turn has to be taken to a safe house with her grandson. And we have this young woman being holed up in fear of her life, and all because of what your friend Jon Reznick did. It's illegal, it's outrageous, and we're paying the price for it."

Raymond Sears, director of Homeland Security, cleared his throat. "Martha, Director O'Donoghue is absolutely correct. The ripples are a cause for concern. Not least because Cain and this militia are so dangerous."

Meyerstein glanced at her notes as she felt the

sweat run down her back. "I can't disagree with either of you. What you say is transparently correct. What I would say, though, is that whilst these ripples are a cause for concern, they have inadvertently given us a possible insight into what we are facing. Namely, militia leader Hunter Cain clearly aligned with two prominent Aryan Brotherhood guys, years and years ago. And the analysis I have, and which has been sent to you and should be in front of you, is that what began as perhaps an affiliation, has deepened inside Leavenworth, so much so that a spectacular might very well be in the offing."

Sears stared down from the screens.

"This would leverage the number of contacts and other assets which could be used, be they safe houses, personnel, training, funding et cetera. The escape from Leavenworth was planned with military precision. Both these AB guys were at one time in the army. Not for long. But they were there. Cain is a former Delta operator. Elite. Highly dangerous. Trained to kill. Bomb. Maim."

O'Donoghue said, "Martha, let's leave that aside just now. Death threats to Kathleen Burke, and her and her family having to flee, are a direct result of Jon Reznick. Both Director Sears and myself want him off your team with immediate effect."

Meyerstein said nothing as she felt the eyes from the screen bear down on her.

Sears said, "Martha, there isn't a cat's chance in

hell that we could defend having Reznick on the team, especially now. If we let him go now, what's done is done and we can move on."

Meyerstein said, "Sir, I've had this conversation before. And I take on board both your views. And I welcome the opportunity to discuss this role, or how we can redefine it in the future. But I do feel this is not the best moment."

Sears said, "Martha, he's gotta go. And now. Otherwise ..."

"Otherwise what, sir?"

Sears cleared his throat. "Otherwise I'll have to step in and recommend formally to Director O'Donoghue that you should be relieved of your duties."

Meyerstein felt as if she had been hit hard in the guts. She felt winded. Knocked off balance.

"Your call. But it's got to be the right call. And just for the sake of argument, the right call is for Reznick to be removed from this investigation forthwith."

Meyerstein said nothing. She mulled over her response.

O'Donoghue leaned forward. "Martha, I for one believe Jon Reznick contributed to your previous investigations. But I think this incident has proven that it's gone too far. We can't have such an operative working in conjunction on an investigation. The methods are different. The MO is different. Ends don't justify means in our book. But clearly Jon Reznick has not read that memo."

Meyerstein's mind was racing. She thought of her father. How he would respond. She remembered him saying that expediency is bullshit. Stand on your own feet. And if the powers-that-be don't like it, fuck 'em. "Director O'Donoghue and Director Sears, I'd like, if I may, to clarify my position."

Sears and O'Donoghue shrugged.

"Whilst the means Reznick used can't be condoned, and I certainly wouldn't try to, I'm not going to throw him overboard. Not now. Not ever."

Both men looked stunned.

"You wanna know why?"

"Sometimes, just sometimes, you need people like Jon Reznick in your corner. He's in our corner, my corner right now, and I will not have his name trashed by you or anyone."

Sears held up his hands as if to pacify her. "Martha, it might be better if …"

"I don't want to hear any of it. He's in, and that's it. You don't like it, then you'll just have to fire me. Okay?"

O'Donoghue said, "Listen to me …"

"He stays. I don't do walking away. Not in the middle of an investigation. That's not the way I do things. So, if it bothers you so much, you're going to have to either live with this or fire my ass. Am I making myself clear?"

Sears said, "Meyerstein, you've crossed the line."

"Have I? Big deal. You come to me with complaints about process, procedures and illegality. I acknowledge aspects of this investigation aren't ideal. But we are where we are. And I believe we are further on than we were."

O'Donoghue said, "Martha, we're no further forward. Not an inch."

"With respect, sir, that's not true. We have two AB nuts who had dropped off the radar at the same time as Cain escapes. How do we know this? Simply because we joined up the dots from what Kathleen Burke knew. This has been conceived inside Leavenworth. And we've got something to work with."

A silence opened up over the videoconference.

"So, there it is. We move forward. If you don't want me to move forward with this, you'll have to fire me. Is that what you want?"

O'Donoghue and Sears were both silent.

"Very well. I'll take that as confirmation that the investigation continues. Good afternoon, gentlemen."

THIRTEEN

Reznick was drinking a coffee, discussing the coded letter with gang expert Ed Forlain, when Meyerstein walked into the room. She was carrying a coffee. "Ed's just giving me a lowdown on this AB prison code."

Meyerstein sipped her coffee. "Tell me more, Ed."

"Here's the thing. The Aryan Brotherhood have not just got some of the nastiest bastards behind bars, highly violent individuals who account for twenty-five percent of all the murders in American penitentiaries, despite only amounting to three percent of the prison population. What's also disturbing about them is the level of sophistication."

Reznick said, "Ed, tell Assistant Director Meyerstein what you just told me."

"The language they've used in this letter, found at one of their houses, is classic AB. But it's couched in code. Let me read direct from it." Forlain turned and looked at his screen. *I am a father at last. It's a boy. My wife gave birth to a strapping eight pound seven ounce baby boy.*

Reznick said, "Seems pretty innocuous on the surface."

Forlain smiled. "That's the whole point, Jon. Firstly, let's break it down. *It's a boy* is their way of saying they have official authorization to launch a war. If they didn't have that authorization, the message would be *It's a girl*."

Reznick said, "This was sent from California. This is from the AB leadership in California?"

"Almost certainly. Here's a very, very interesting aspect. I've only had half an hour to look at this, but I think we've got something. The reference to the weight of the baby is very important."

"How?"

"There are three separate quantities."

"So what are they?"

"The word 'a' before boy refers to the number 1. Then '8' and '7'. Separately they mean nothing. But use some lateral thinking, a knowledge of the law, and you can conceal the real message. It's referring to California Penal Code 187, and the crime of murder."

Reznick said, "So this is, in your opinion, one hundred percent, the authorization from the Aryan Brotherhood to go ahead with a murder?"

"No question."

Meyerstein said nothing for a few moments.

Reznick said, "Okay, we now have concrete proof of this guy's involvement, the authorization from the AB. The question that still needs to be answered is, what's the target and where's the destination?"

Meyerstein finished the rest of her coffee and stared at the screen. "There's obviously a common thread that has brought the AB and this militia together. Ideology? Is there a target they can both agree on?"

Reznick said, "Ed, you know about gangs, especially this one. What are their trigger points?"

"Blacks. Authority. Government."

"And the militia, their major problem is what?"

Meyerstein said, "The government. Big business. Remember McVeigh took out the FBI in Oklahoma. The Federal Building. Could we be talking about the same thing?"

Reznick said, "What's the latest analysis showing?"

Meyerstein said, "I'm hooking up with a joint terrorism taskforce in DC who are analyzing this. Hopefully someone can give me an answer, or we have a developing problem on our hands."

FOURTEEN

Kathleen Burke dragged hard on a cigarette in the living room of the FBI safe house, daytime TV on with the sound off. She turned and looked across at one of the special agents guarding her. "I don't like it here."

Agent Limez said, "Why not? No one knows you're here. You've got everything you need."

Burke shook her head. "I don't know. I just don't like it. Feels like I'm going out of my mind."

Limez said, "Have you had your methadone, Kathleen? Maybe that would help."

"I've had my fucking methadone, thank you. And I still feel like I'm crawling the walls. I can't bear it. Feel like I'm trapped." She dragged heavily on her cigarette again. "The curtains and blinds are all drawn. I want to be outside in the sun."

Limez said, "Kathleen, we've got to be focussed here. We can't have you out and about at this time."

Burke leaned over and crushed out the cigarette in a glass ashtray. "So when can I get out? I can't stay here forever, can I?"

Limez said nothing.

"And don't fucking stare at me like that."

"Kathleen, I'm not staring at you. You need to calm down."

Burke felt helpless and out of control. "No, I won't fucking calm down. I want to get out and into the sunshine. Is that asking too much?"

Limez sighed and looked at her long and hard. He then pulled out his cellphone from his jacket pocket and punched in a number. "Ma'am, sorry to bother you … but Ms Burke is insisting she leaves the premises." He nodded. "Yes, I explained that." He handed the cellphone to Burke. "Assistant Director Meyerstein wants to talk to you."

Burke took the phone. "Yeah, I'm going crazy here."

Meyerstein said, "Listen to me, Kathleen, you're safe there. It's important that you stay on the premises and keep out of sight till this dies down."

"And when the hell will that be?"

"I don't know is the honest answer."

"You don't know? So what am I supposed to do? Just sit around here for the next year, is that it?"

"Kathleen, what exactly do you want?"

"I want out. I want the sun on my face. I want to chill the fuck out. I want a beer."

"We can get you a beer. But it's important you stay out of sight for now."

Burke closed her eyes and felt tears rolling down her cheeks. "I'm scared. I don't like this. Please … What do I do?"

"You're fine, Kathleen. Look, I'll send a doctor across and get you some medication to make you feel better for now, how about that?"

"Yeah, whatever."

Burke ended the call, stared at the TV and began to cry.

FIFTEEN

When Meyerstein emerged from the video-conference room, Jon Reznick was waiting for her. He walked down the corridor toward her as she carried a pile of briefing papers. He thought she looked exhausted, dark shadows under her eyes.

"You okay?" he said.

"Nothing I can't handle."

"Your boss giving you a hard time?"

"Like I said, nothing I can't handle."

"They wanted you to fire my ass, right?"

"I can't discuss that, Jon."

Reznick grinned. "You know, Meyerstein, you really are something."

Meyerstein flushed. "Yeah, well …"

"So what's the latest?"

Meyerstein sighed. "We're on the move."

"Where?"

"Vero Beach on the east coast of Florida."

"Why?"

"Just got intel about a guy who knew Hunter inside Leavenworth."

"What else?"

"Hunter killed this guy's friend in cold blood. His boyfriend."

Reznick said nothing.

"Guy's name in Vero Beach is Jimmy Samson."

"What else?"

"We're going to fly down there and see what he has to say."

A few hours later, the SUV with Reznick, Meyerstein and two other Feds inside pulled up outside a trailer on the outskirts of Vero Beach.

Reznick followed Meyerstein. She knocked three times on the door. The door opened and a tattooed guy wearing a vest was sitting in a wheelchair.

Meyerstein flashed her badge. "Jimmy Samson?"

He stared at the badge for a few moments. "What's this about?"

Reznick said, "We need to talk in private."

Samson cocked his head and they went inside while the two Feds stayed behind in the car. "Take a seat."

Meyerstein sat down on the made-up sofa bed as Reznick stayed standing.

Samson shrugged. "I'm clean. I did my time. Okay, I don't want trouble or anything."

Reznick said, "Jimmy, you can rest easy on that. We're looking for help locating a guy you used to know."

Samson winced. "Man, don't be giving me all that stuff."

"Jimmy, I'm gonna be straight with you. I was reading your file. And we know you have MS, and I'm sorry about that."

Samson said nothing.

"Jimmy, we're looking for Hunter Cain."

"What are you talking about? He's inside. Leavenworth still, right?"

"Not anymore, Jimmy."

"Bullshit."

"Afraid not. Managed to escape. And we believe he's in Florida."

Samson closed his eyes and shook his head. "Fucking hell."

"Now I'm gonna be upfront. We don't know where Hunter is. No one does."

"Neither do I. And I'm not likely to if you know anything about me."

Reznick nodded. "Jimmy, I read about what he did to your partner, Alfredo."

Samson winced at the mention of the memory.

"Hunter stabbed him to death, didn't he?"

Samson began to sob. "Please … I don't want any trouble."

"There's no trouble, Jimmy. All we want is to try and find out if there's anything you know about Hunter Cain. You were quite tight with his crew."

"Yeah, well that was before Alfredo got shanked. I became an outcast as he was my friend."

"Hunter didn't like gays, right?"

Samson bowed his head and nodded. "I think they were gonna do the same to me so I asked to get moved to solitary."

"Tell me what you know about Hunter from your time inside."

Samson looked across at Meyerstein, who smiled back. "You really assistant director of the FBI?"

Meyerstein said, "Yes I am, for my sins."

Samson gave a wry smile. He let out a long sigh. "Hunter Cain is crazy. Scared the fuck out of me from the first moment I saw him. Just had that evil look in his eyes, you know what I'm saying?"

Reznick said nothing.

"He didn't know I was gay. I didn't tell anyone. It just wasn't what was done with those guys."

"What do you mean, 'those guys'?"

"The Aryan Brotherhood psychopaths who hung around Hunter. I was on the periphery of their crowd. I'm white, as you can see, and I naturally gravitated towards my own race inside – it's natural, trust me."

"What sort of person was he? Did he have any fixations?"

Samson went quiet for a few moments. "He carried a picture of his mother and father around with him. I kinda liked that about him when we met."

Reznick said, "I believe Hunter was brought up by foster parents."

"The pictures were of his biological parents. I remember I once saw him put the pictures up on the wall of his cell. And then he, like, broke down. It was pretty bad to see."

"He didn't know you were watching?"

"I don't think so. I was just passing by his cell."

"I remember a friend of his said Hunter's dad became an alcoholic. Couldn't afford the rent of his house after the bank foreclosed. And his father started drinking. Drinking real hard."

Reznick nodded.

"His mother took Hunter away and she got jobs cleaning. Had four jobs at one time, cleaning big houses."

"So what happened after that?"

"She had a breakdown, got committed to an asylum. Hunter was taken into care. Father killed himself a short while later."

Reznick looked down at Samson. "Anything else you can remember?"

"Like what?"

"I don't know – you tell me."

Samson ran his hand through his hair. Let out a long sigh. "Nothing I can remember."

Meyerstein stepped forward and handed him her card. "If you remember anything give me a call, night or day."

SIXTEEN

Hunter Cain and the two AB operatives were escorted to the attic apartment just off Washington Avenue. Three mattresses in one room, air-con unit growling low in the background. The blinds were shut and they had pizza, a large bottle of Coke delivered by one of the back-up crew, an iPad and an iPhone.

"Enjoy your evening," the crew guy said before carefully heading downstairs and driving off in his small hatchback.

Cain and the guys scoffed the pizza and washed it down with gulps of the Coke. Feeling better, Cain switched on the iPad. An email was waiting for him. He clicked on it and a map appeared. He turned the iPad to show his two colleagues. "This is the layout of the building. Six floors high, two below ground. Stairwells, fire escapes, ceiling heights, everything."

Neil said, "How many are there going to be?"

"Couple hundred, maybe more."

Neil grinned. "How long till we go?"

"Two days and two nights. We're in position. And we're gonna have a ball, right?"

Cain switched on his cellphone. It began to ring almost immediately.

"I believe you gentlemen are now at base camp," a familiar voice said. It was the handler.

Cain stared at his two accomplices. "We're here. And we're good."

"Good is what we like to hear. Okay, I won't keep you too long. From our side of the fence, it's looking good. We're happy with the arrangements. And it's coming together. The switch of venue hasn't been revealed, but when it is, it'll be in lockdown. But we have contingency plans already in place."

"What about our IDs, our clothes, weapons, where and how? I need details."

"All in good time. It's all in hand. Tell me, one final thing, how are your two friends?"

"In what way?"

"Are they showing nerves?"

"Not at all. They're solid."

"And you?"

"What about me?"

"How do you feel?"

"I feel nothing. That's why this is a piece of cake for me."

"I knew you were the one, Hunter. Till the next time …"

The line went dead.

SEVENTEEN

The sun was low in the sky, and the sky the color of blood. Reznick was sitting on the sand as Meyerstein walked alone on the sands at Vero Beach. She had her cellphone pressed to her ear. He could see the investigation wasn't going well. Anyone could see that. And he wondered if it was all getting to her.

He could only imagine the pressure she was working under. The more he thought of it, the more he realized she had a myriad of aspects to consider.

Reznick turned and looked back – saw the two Feds standing beside the SUV, keeping watch over her. His gaze wandered down the beach. He saw Meyerstein had ended the call and was staring out at the ocean.

Reznick got up and wandered down the beach to be beside her. He saw tears were streaming down her face. "What is it?"

"Nothing."

"It's not nothing, Meyerstein."

Meyerstein dabbed her eyes. "I got a message from my mother. She's looking after the kids. She's more or less moved in with me. And she was asking how I was. But she said my daughter was asking when I'd be back. I'm just off the phone to her. And I couldn't answer. I just said, 'Mommy will be home as soon as she can. I promise.'"

Reznick said nothing.

"Anyway, nothing I can do about that, is there?"

"We've all got choices."

"You think I should just give up my job, career and head back to the house, is that it?"

"That's not it. I just said we've all got choices. And as it stands, you've chosen your career."

"But you're implying that if I want to see more of my kids I've got to get back into the home."

"Meyerstein, we've all got tough choices to make. You're away from your kids as they're growing up. It's tough. I know. I was away when Lauren was growing up. She's still away from me. But you know what? Kids are more resilient than you think."

"I don't feel very resilient today."

Reznick nodded and turned and faced the ocean.

"You think I'm weak, don't you?"

Reznick shook his head. "No I don't. Quite the opposite, actually."

Meyerstein took a long sigh and blew out her cheeks. "I'm my own worst enemy. I'm working sixteen-hour days. I'm away from my children, my family, all the goddamn time. Never seem to find a moment, you know what I mean?"

Reznick said nothing.

"What about you?"

"What about me?"

"How do you cope when things aren't going your way?"

Reznick took a few moments to think about his answer. "I tend to compartmentalize. Enjoy time by myself."

Meyerstein said, "Huh."

"Yeah, not much of an answer, I know."

"It's very interesting how men seem much more able to deal with stuff like that."

"We're wired differently."

"Are you?"

"Sure."

"Maybe you're right." She sighed. "Jon, we're nowhere on this. And I'm getting it from all sides, believe me. They're looking for results and we're not getting any. I can't seem to get a break on this."

Reznick gave a wry smile.

"What is it?"

"Sometimes, just sometimes, you need to look at it in a different light."

Meyerstein shrugged.

"You say we're nowhere on this case. I disagree. I think we're building up a picture of Hunter Cain. I didn't know half what we know."

Meyerstein shook her head. "We're nowhere."

"We've just not joined up the dots. We're beginning to."

"It's the endgame. We're missing the endgame."

"But before the endgame, we need to get some more pieces of the jigsaw in place."

Meyerstein sighed. "My father's a lawyer. He often talked about the importance of building a case from the ground up. Get a solid foundation to an understanding of the case. And from that, everything follows."

"What are counter-terrorism saying?"

"They're coming at this cold ... Florida is a big place, they say. Anti-government militia targets? Honestly? They don't know. They're scratching their heads, trying to figure it out. One or two saying there's nothing in the offing."

"What do you think?"

"I think they're wrong. There absolutely is something in the offing."

Reznick nodded.

"Give me some of your thoughts, Jon."

The sun dipped over the horizon as the sky went a dark crimson. "What was the point in springing Hunter Cain from a top-security penitentiary unless something's planned?"

Meyerstein nodded.

"Whoever's behind this doesn't want to have him on the outside for no reason. The people behind it, and I believe there are people behind this, believe he can advance their aims. He has top-quality military skills. Organization, leadership, technical, the works. I believe the mission has been known about for some time. And he's escaped just before this event's planned. Maybe a matter of days. Maybe hours. They couldn't risk having Hunter Cain on the loose for months. He might get caught. No, something's going down, and going down very soon."

"I thought it very interesting the revelation that Cain's father, his biological father, killed himself. It'd be useful to know more about that. And I've got Stamper and his team to look into that."

"I worked alongside Hunter for years. And in all the time, I didn't know anything about that."

"You said before he was sadistic."

"Yeah ... real mean motherfucker."

Meyerstein's cellphone rang. "Never a goddamn minute." She closed her eyes for a moment before answering. "Yeah?" She nodded. "Are we sure?" She listened for a few moments. "We're heading down. Good work." She ended the call.

"Who was that?"

"Face-recognition software has pulled up the face of Ken 'Mad Dog' Pearce at a 7-Eleven in South Beach."

"Miami is the locale."

Meyerstein stared at him long and hard. "Let's get down there. We've got a lot of work to do."

EIGHTEEN

Kathleen Burke stood in the living room of the safe house, blinds drawn, shaking as she popped her methadone pill and washed it down with a gulp of beer. She looked across at the two Feds watching her. "So is this how it's gonna be, huh?"

One Fed said, "You've got your meds, we've got some beers in for you – just kick back and relax. You're fine."

"I'm fine? Do I look fine to you? Do I?"

The Fed averted his gaze.

"No I fucking don't. I know what I look like. A fucking mess. A walking, talking piece of trash. That's what they call me. I know what they say behind my back."

"Kathleen, I think you need to remember what the doctor said. You need to rest. And you need to calm down."

"Rest? You think rest is what I need? You Feds, you're something else. You don't know about me. Don't fucking pretend you do."

The Fed said nothing as his colleague shifted in a seat in the corner.

Burke finished the rest of the beer. She got another cold one from the fridge and took a long gulp. "This is the only thing that will calm me down."

"The doctor recommended you don't mix too much booze with the medication."

"What do doctors know?"

The Fed sighed.

"I want to see my mother and my kids. When can I see them?"

"We've got protocols. This is not the right moment."

"At least let me speak to them."

"That's not gonna happen. Look, you're safe here, right?"

"What the fuck does that mean? My ex-boy-friend is a psychopath. He called my mother. This ain't gonna end good."

"You're safe."

"You reckon? Let me tell you, Hunter Cain can reach anyone, anywhere, at any time. I know only too well what he's like."

Burke sat down and opened a beer, taking a long gulp. It felt good. "Goddamn."

The Fed said, "Look, Kathleen, you need to focus. And cool it."

Burke felt the tears begin to well up in her eyes and her throat tighten. "What a fucking mess I am."

The Fed said nothing, gaze averted.

"Look at me."

The Fed looked across the room at her. "What?"

"I want to speak to Meyerstein."

"Not possible."

"Listen, I want to talk to her."

The Fed sighed and shook his head. "Why?"

"I want to tell her how I feel."

"Look, I've told you …"

"Are you gonna let me speak to her or not?"

The Fed sighed and headed into the kitchen. She heard his voice on the phone, explaining the situation. Then he came back into the living room and handed her the phone. "Assistant Director Meyerstein. You've got a minute."

Burke took the phone. "Meyerstein, I don't like being holed up like this. I want somewhere different."

Meyerstein said, "Kathleen, now just relax. You've got everything you need there. Medication and whatever else, right?"

"I feel sick. I want to see my kids. My mother. I want to call them."

"Not possible."

"What do you mean, not possible?"

"There can be no contact till this is over."

"And when will that be?"

Meyerstein said nothing.

"See … you don't know yourself when this whole thing will end. I could be stuck here for months."

"That's not going to be the case, Kathleen."

"Well, how long?"

A silence opened up down the line. "Maybe a few days. Maybe a week or so."

"I'm going out of my mind here."

"Listen, how about we get a new doctor sent round, and he can get your mood lifted – how does that sound? It might be what you need. Do you suffer from anxiety?"

"Yeah. Big time. And this isn't helping."

"Leave it with me. I'll get a doctor and maybe he can help you out."

Burke felt tears spill down her face. "I'm sorry … you must think I'm pathetic."

"You're not pathetic, Kathleen. This is a terrible situation you're in. But we're here to help you. And protect you and your family. Don't ever forget that."

NINETEEN

Matt Pearce pulled up a block from the waterfront house where the Feds had Kathleen Burke. Exterior security lights, and lights on upstairs. He switched off his engine and checked the GPS tracking app on his iPhone. It showed Burke inside the smart house with a Lincoln parked outside. He took a note of the license plate and relayed that back.

He wondered who was inside with her. Was it friends? Boyfriends? Was it their car outside? His instructions had been simple. *Find her. Watch her. And then kill her.*

He knew he had to comply with the request. It was made by Hunter Cain no less. He'd served time with him, along with his brother, in Leavenworth. Aryan Brotherhood had certain codes of honor. Blood flowed. And it always flowed with the AB. He knew if he didn't carry out the order, he'd be killed himself. As would his brother. No ifs or buts. It was just the way it was.

And that was fine. He knew they'd be there for him.

Since he'd been released, he'd killed three people

on orders from Cain. A former AB guy who had turned informer. A Texas skinhead who hadn't carried out a planned hit. And a black guy dealing methamphetamines to white kids in a trailer park.

He hadn't thought twice about any of the hits. It was AB business. And that's all he needed to know.

He wondered how he should execute her. Would he break in and just blast her? Stab her when she went to the pharmacy for her meds?

The more he thought about it, the more excited he got.

He felt his guts tighten and his heart start to race. The endorphins were kicking in. He sensed this was going to be a good one.

His cellphone vibrated in his shirt pocket, snapping him out of his reverie.

"Matt, you in place?" The voice was Hunter Cain.

"Maybe fifty yards or so from the house, bro."

"Any sign of her?"

"Too early. Just got here."

A long sigh down the line. "Okay, good work. I owe you one for this, buddy."

"The car outside. The Lincoln."

"Yeah."

"Feds."

Cain took a few moments to answer. "You reckon you can handle this?"

"It's all in hand, bro."

"Want it dealt with real quick."

"How quick?"

"Sooner rather than later."

"Leave it with me."

The line went dead.

TWENTY

Reznick was in the back of an FBI Lincoln headed down I-95 when Meyerstein's cellphone rang. She covered the mouthpiece and clicked her fingers to get his attention. She whispered, *It's him.*

He knew exactly who it would be.

Reznick took the cellphone from her. "Yeah, who's this?"

A long silence opened up before a man spoke. "Jon Reznick ... well, I'll be damned."

Reznick recognized the voice and accent immediately. "Hunter, how you doing?"

"How am I doing? I'm doing great, man. I got a message from a woman to give you a call. Didn't realize you were employed by the FBI now ... you've changed, man."

Reznick stared out of the window. "I heard you got out and I was wanting to talk."

Cain sighed long and hard. "Sorry to say, bro, don't believe a goddamn word you're saying. Wish it wasn't so. But, hey, it happens to the best of us, right?"

"Hunter, hear me out. You didn't just escape prison to enjoy the Florida sun, did you?"

"Are you fucking judging me? Are you casting aspersions on a former Delta buddy? You working for the government? Are you kidding me?"

"I'm not working for the government. I'm working with them to ensure that whatever it is you have in mind doesn't escalate."

"Jon, I've never had no beef with you, man. I love you, man. Like a brother, you know that. But sometimes, just sometimes, a man has to take sides."

"It's not about sides, Hunter. It's about doing the right thing."

"The right thing, huh?"

Reznick looked at Meyerstein, who was leaning forward and whispering in the lead Fed's right ear. "I just wanna talk."

"Jon, the time for talking ended a long, long time ago. You know that better than anyone. I know what you think of the government. The country. You think it's going to the dogs, don't you?"

"I think we need to do a lot of things a helluva lot better. And, yes, we need to keep the hell out of people's lives."

"Jon, you've spoken to my girlfriend, right?"

"Yes I did."

"Jon, I want to be really upfront with you. I'm going to kill her. And I'm going to kill anyone who gets in my way. And that goes for you!"

"Hunter, this doesn't have to go down, whatever it is you're planning."

"Ah, but that's where you're wrong, Jon. This has to go down. Why? Because Americans need to realize that we're no longer in charge of our country. It's the government. It's the banks. It's the institutions. The little guy doesn't stand a chance. We need to try and reclaim back what is rightfully ours."

"Hunter, I don't disagree with anything you've just said. But once you cross a line into killing innocents, you've lost the right to your point of view."

"Jon … be under no illusion. I'm going to kill my girlfriend. And I'm going to make people sit up and take notice of what's happening to our country, right under our fucking noses."

"Why won't you meet up and talk it over?"

"Man, you're just a patsy. A government patsy, Jon. I love you, man. But I'm gonna kill you too if you get in my way."

Reznick said nothing.

"Don't fuck with me, man. Don't ever fuck with me."

Then the line went dead.

TWENTY-ONE

Meyerstein stared out of the window of the SUV. She felt a renewed sense of trepidation after the call from Hunter Cain. The investigation was slipping out from her control. The pressure from above – the director of the FBI and the director of Homeland Security – only added to a sense that she hadn't got a grip of events. Things were sliding.

When they pulled up at Pompano Beach for a coffee break, Meyerstein headed out onto the sands alone. She began to walk and walk as the breakers crashed onto the shore. It felt good to get the warm sea air and the sun on her skin. What she wouldn't give for a two-week vacation. She never seemed to find the time.

The more she thought of it the more alone she felt. She was surrounded by people all throughout the day. But it was work. Constant. From sunup to sunset. Relentless. Sometimes around the clock.

She thought of her family being looked after by her mother at her house in Bethesda. On the surface it was idyllic. The great job. The great house. The beautiful children. But since her husband had left her, she'd noticed a sadness seep into her thoughts. She was getting more and introspective. She didn't want to enjoy lunches with friends. She was immersing herself so much in work that she wasn't giving herself or her family any time.

She remembered her father saying that one of his biggest regrets was never finding the time to be a father when Martha was growing up. Instead, the would-be partner in a powerful Chicago law firm was working sixteen-hour days, seven days a week. He didn't have time for family. He drove himself hard. To the top. But he also missed out on the great things children do. School Christmas plays, fun days at the beach, weekends at home. Even in his sixties, he was still doing seventy-hour weeks. It was almost like he was scared to slow down in case he lost his position in the firm. She wondered if that was her problem. If she slowed down there would be some-one else to take her place.

Meyerstein could see she was becoming more and more like her father. She took out her cellphone and punched in her home number. Her mother answered. It was good to hear her soft voice. Yes, the kids were great. They were at school. When was she coming home? Hopefully soon. She ended the call and punched in her father's cellphone number. He answered on the fifth ring. "Hey, dad, how's it going?"

"Martha, honey, I'm great. Mom's missing you. Are you okay?"

Meyerstein felt her eyes fill with tears. She missed

hearing his voice. "Dad ... I'm good, thanks. Work's just kinda, well, you know ..."

He went quiet for a few moments as if waiting to pick the correct words to use. "Martha, I can hear in your tone of voice something's wrong. I can hear it, honey. Because I know you. Tell me what's wrong. I've got all the time in the world for you today."

Meyerstein dabbed her eyes and shielded them from the sun. She turned round. In the distance Reznick was standing outside the SUV, drinking a coffee, looking in her direction. She gave a wave of acknowledgment and he did the same. She turned round and stared out over the ocean. "I'm getting a lot of heat."

"What kind of heat?"

"The kind of heat that involves using the services of a certain operative."

"You talking about Mr R?"

Meyerstein smiled. "The very one."

A long sigh down the line. "Martha, you've told me quite a lot about him. And I've thought about that. You've told me about what he's done for you. And I've got to say, I admit I've never met him, but I think you've deployed him judiciously."

"My bosses don't feel the same way. They're threatening me with 'it's either you or him.'"

Her father sighed down the line. "What do you want to do?"

"I know what he can do. I know what he can

bring. And I know he crosses lines, boundaries and God knows what else. And this can be problematic."

"Is he breaking laws?"

"He has."

"Not good."

"I know. Thing is, his actions, they break some federal laws, but he's helped us get a handle on a developing situation."

"You talking about a few eggs getting broken, sort of thing?"

"Precisely."

"The problem is, once you start ignoring illegality, before long it becomes the norm. Besides, you're in the law-enforcement business, right?"

"Broadly speaking, yes."

"Martha, want my advice?"

"Sure."

"You gotta draw a line in the sand with him. Have that conversation. But then move on."

"But my boss, he doesn't see it like that. I believe they're not bluffing when they say they'll get rid of me. I've taken years and years of damned hard work to get where I am."

"I know that better than anyone, Martha. So, my question to you is, what are you going to do?"

"I'm going to have to think long and hard about that."

Meyerstein turned round and saw one of her team signaling that they were on the move. "Dad, I gotta go. Thanks for that. I love you."

"Love you too, honey."

Meyerstein ended the call and turned and headed along the beach to the car. She slid in the back beside Reznick.

"You okay?" he asked.

"I'm fine." She leaned forward and tapped the driver on the shoulder. "Let's get down to the FBI field office in Miami. Step on it."

TWENTY-TWO

Just after midnight, Hunter Cain emerged from the unfurnished apartment on 14th Street and walked across the street to the Deuce bar, a windowless dive. He'd been holed up for the last twelve hours and was getting cabin fever. He walked in and ordered a vodka and Coke. He looked around, saw a smattering of hipsters, alcoholics and a few nice-looking chicks. Rock music playing loud.

Cain ignored it all. Had a timetable to adhere to. A plan. Bit by bit was coming into place. His two accomplices had moved to a separate studio apartment on Washington as arranged. A few minutes later they walked in. He ignored them as Mad Dog ordered a couple of bottles of Schlitz. He caught their eye, turned and headed to the bathroom. It was empty.

A few moments later Pearce came in. He handed the new cellphone to Cain.

"Good work," Cain said. "Any problems?"

Pearce shook his head. "What time you expecting the call?"

"Fifteen minutes."

"You follow me as soon as I leave the bar, right?"

"Got it."

Cain returned to the bar as Pearce returned to his position at the far end. He ordered a Heineken. The cold beer felt good.

His cellphone vibrated in his pocket and he took it out.

"Listen and listen good, Hunter. You don't know me, but I know you. This is how it's going to work. There's an alley down the side of the bar."

"Yeah, I saw it."

"There's a cab waiting for you. A second one is out front on 14th Street for your two friends."

"Where exactly are we going?"

"Not long now, Hunter, relax."

The line went dead.

TWENTY-THREE

Reznick was sitting in the back of the SUV with Meyerstein as they approached the outskirts of Miami. Stamper sat up front with the driver. "How long till we're at the field office?"

The driver said, "Fifteen minutes, once we get through this goddamn traffic."

Stamper turned round and looked at Reznick. "Jon, tell me more about Hunter Cain. We've been over his records. Military and all that. Prison. But what I'm puzzled at is you had no inkling your old Delta buddy was in jail."

"Why would I know what he was up to?"

"I don't know … I thought all you guys stuck together. Thought you were tight."

"We are. But people don't keep in touch with everyone they know. Do you keep in touch with all your friends at college?"

Stamper flushed. "No, but college is different."

"Is it? How is it different?"

"Jon, I'm merely asking a civil question. I wish to God you wouldn't be so defensive."

"You wanna know about Hunter Cain? Read his file."

"I have. But I thought you could enlighten me as to how one of your fellow Delta operators could have gone so badly off the rails."

"Roy, here's the thing. We're trained to kill. It's sometimes not so easy for some people to switch all that off."

"Are you condoning him?"

"Don't be so fucking stupid."

Meyerstein's cellphone rang and she put up her hand as if to silence them. "Enough!" She answered the call. "Yeah, Martha speaking." She scrunched up her face. "Are you kidding me? Seriously? That's ridiculous." She ended the call.

Reznick looked at her. "What is it?"

"That was the FBI field office in Miami. They've received instructions from the director that Jon Reznick is not to be admitted to the premises."

Reznick said nothing.

Meyerstein sighed. "This is getting ridiculous. We're in the middle of a goddamn investigation and they're pulling stunts like that. It's crazy."

Stamper turned round. "Martha, for what it's worth, I think …"

"Roy, enough! I need to think."

Meyerstein tapped the driver on the shoulder. "How far from North Miami Beach to Miami-Dade police HQ?"

"Twenty minutes."

"Let's get to it."

★

As they headed across town, Reznick felt a growing sense of unease. He wondered if Meyerstein was crossing the line and putting herself up against powerful forces within the highest echelons of the American intelligence community. When he tried to raise these points, she brushed them aside. Instead, Meyerstein called in a favor with the Miami-Dade police chief she knew, and they pitched up in a secure meeting room. It was almost like she was wanting the confrontation with the directors of the FBI and Homeland Security.

Reznick was introduced to Lee Jackson, a police officer who specialized in Florida gangs and militias. He had the lowdown on biker groups, Hell's Angels, Aryan Brotherhood associates and militias across the state. He told them that white gangs had become all-pervasive, especially with the spread of methamphetamine dealing. He told them about biker gangs who owed the militias money. And he told them about a failed hit on a militia associate the previous year.

The image of Mad Dog Pearce was uploaded to a huge TV screen.

"Roy, give me details about exactly when and where this was taken before we open this up," Meyerstein said.

"This guy is one of Hunter Cain's most trusted associates. High propensity to extreme violence. Not afraid to mix it with anyone. But, anyway, this was taken at a 7-Eleven at Alton Road and 15th

Street, twelve hours ago. As you can see he's carrying a 7-Eleven bag. According to the manager he bought two sandwiches, two Cokes, two candy bars and two packets of cigarettes."

Meyerstein nodded and looked at the gang officer. "You want to speculate, Jackson?"

"Question is, where's the other one?"

Reznick said, "Roy, have we got any other footage of this guy?"

"That's it."

"So the question is, is Hunter Cain with this guy Pearce, or is there anyone else? Also, are they all together?"

Stamper scrunched up his face. "Why would they split up?"

"If one gets caught, for example Pearce, it doesn't bring down the whole operation."

Meyerstein nodded. "Cell structure?"

"Basically, yeah," Reznick said. "We got lucky with this clip of Pearce. But if that camera hadn't been working at that time, we'd have nothing. If I was in Cain's shoes, I'd make sure I was apart from the others."

Meyerstein looked across at Jackson. "You think they were hunkered down there. Do you think they might still be there?"

Jackson blew out his cheeks. "Possibly. Who the hell knows what these guys are planning? That's part of the problem. We don't know what they're up to."

Reznick said, "Hunter Cain is not a stupid man. He'll know it's only a matter of time till they're tracked down. So that's why they won't be sticking around for long."

Meyerstein glanced up at the image of Pearce on the big screen. Then she stared across at Roy. "What's the latest analysis we're getting from your team on this?"

"It's all pointing to one thing. Miami, clearly."

"Okay, I get that, but exactly what? What's going to go down?"

Reznick leaned back in his seat. "Roy, we know about this message that was smuggled out. The assassination code. But we need to be further along the line with analysis at this stage, don't we?"

Stamper stood and pointed at Reznick. "Who the hell do you think you're speaking to?"

"It's a simple question, Roy, and you don't seem to be able to answer it."

"I don't answer to you, you understand?"

Meyerstein stared long and hard at Reznick before she fixed her gaze on Stamper. "No. But you do answer to me, Roy. So where are we with this?"

Stamper slumped back down into his seat. "We have nothing. Hunter Cain and his guys are out there, and we don't have a clue where they are at this moment, or what they're about to do."

An icy silence descended on the room.

Meyerstein's cellphone began to ring. She picked up. "Who's this?" She nodded. "Mr Samson, thanks for taking the time to call back. What is it?" She scribbled some notes. "Are you sure?" She scribbled some more notes. "Now are you positive?" She let out a long sigh and stared across at Reznick. "I appreciate your time, Mr Samson. We'll look into this. Thanks again for your help." She ended the call and leaned back in her seat.

Reznick said, "What is it? He knows something."

Meyerstein nodded. "He said there was something else he forgot to tell us. Something about Hunter that escaped his memory till now."

Stamper shifted in his seat. "What?"

Meyerstein's gaze wandered round the room. "This sounds crazy. He said one night Hunter and his crew were playing cards. And someone asked about his girl. Hunter said she wouldn't fuck around as he knew where she was 24/7."

Stamper said, "That's bullshit."

Meyerstein shook her head. "Sadly not. Remember the cross round Kathleen's neck. Samson said Hunter said he'd got a jeweler friend of his to make a piece of jewelry. A silver cross. And he sent it to her."

Stamper shrugged. "I don't follow."

"Hunter got the jeweler to insert a minuscule GPS sensor inside the cross . It would track her movements, night and day, till he got out."

Stamper shook his head. "Martha, we need to get Kathleen Burke out of the safe house right away!"

Reznick shook his head. "Wrong move, bro."

"What the hell you talking about, Jon? This is not your call."

Reznick looked first at Stamper, then fixed his gaze on Meyerstein. "It sounds like the right play, but it's not. It absolutely is not."

Stamper blew out his cheeks, hands on hips. "Martha, the safe house has been compromised. She needs to move."

"Roy," said Stamper, "think this through. Jesus …"

Meyerstein held up her hand. "Jon, what's your rationale?"

"Rationale? Firstly, we've got to assume they've got someone at this moment aware of where she is. Secondly, we've got to assume they've got someone in place ready to kill her, as Cain said he would. Therefore, logically, it would be harebrained to do anything this overtly."

Meyerstein shrugged. "So what do we do with Kathleen Burke?"

"Get three cars out front. But get one to reverse right up the driveway to a side door. Screen off with a sheet or whatever, tarpaulin. Then get her into the trunk of the second car. And get the hell out of there. We'd effectively have blockers in front and covering the rear. Then get her to a secure facility. Military preferably."

Stamper shook his head. "Jon, with all due respect, that's going to draw attention to matters. It's a bit convoluted."

"If that was my daughter in that situation, that's what I'd do."

Meyerstein got to her feet and began to pace the room. "We need to alert Miami FBI to what we're going to need."

TWENTY-FOUR

Kathleen Burke was on her second packet of cigarettes, drinking a glass of rum and Coke to wash down the methadone, when one of the Feds' phone rang.

The Fed got to his feet and began to pace the room. "Ma'am, I got it. I'll pass that on to her now." He passed Kathleen the cellphone. "Assistant Director Meyerstein for you."

Burke dragged on her cigarette as she took the call, pressing the phone tight to her ear. "Yeah, what is it now?"

"Kathleen, tell me about the cross around your neck."

"What the hell do you want to know about that for? You wanna buy it off me, is that it?"

"No, Kathleen, that's not it. Who gave it you?"

"Why the hell do you wanna know that?" She dragged again on the cigarette and tried to waft the smoke away from the Feds. "What kind of question is that?"

"Answer me, goddamn it!"

Burke was surprised at the sharpness of

Meyerstein's reply. "Man, you really need to dial it down a notch. What is it with you?"

"Kathleen, I'm asking a simple question."

"Yeah, but why are you wanting to know that? Does it matter who gave it to me?"

"Yes, it does. Can you answer my question, please?"

Burke shrugged. "It was Hunter. Hunter gave it me."

"He handed it to you?"

"No, he got a friend of his to deliver it. Thought it was pretty sweet of him. Looks expensive, doesn't it? Hand-made in New York, you believe that?"

"Kathleen, I want you to take it off and hand it to the agent who gave you the phone."

"Fuck off! That's mine! You ain't taking that. Who the fuck do you think you're dealing with?"

"Kathleen, listen to me. We have reason to believe that within the cross is a GPS tracking device."

Burke took a few moments to allow the information to sink into her fuzzy head. "Aw, gimme a goddamn break will you? That's bullshit. What a crock of shit."

"Kathleen, if you don't take it off, I have authorized the federal agent who handed you the phone to take it off you. Are we clear?"

"That's illegal!"

"I'm asking you for your cooperation. Kathleen, do you want me to spell it out for you? Hunter gave you the present so he knew where you were at all times. He could log onto a computer within Leavenworth and check each and every day where you were."

"That's bullshit."

Meyerstein sighed down the line. "You want to find out for sure?"

"This is crazy. Are you saying he'd know I'd been out and about? Where? When?"

"We believe so. That is, if our information is correct. But we need to check."

Burke took the cigarette from her mouth and crushed it in an ashtray. "That's disgusting."

"I know. Can you help us find out for sure?"

Burke felt tears spill down her face. She unhooked the necklace and handed it to the Fed. "I've done that now – happy?"

"Stay on the line …"

Burke slumped in a seat as the Fed prized off the back with a Swiss army knife. She watched him tease off a tiny metal sensor with a pinprick green light on the side, and hold it up. "Motherfucker!"

"Kathleen, was it there?"

"Yes, it goddamn was. Your agent has it now."

"Kathleen, stay on the line. Jon Reznick wants to speak to you."

"What does he want?"

Meyerstein said, "Here he is now."

A deep sigh down the line. "Kathleen, Jon Reznick."

"Everyone having a good laugh at my expense?"

"Not at all, Kathleen. Listen to me, what this means is that you are in grave danger. I have recommended to Assistant Director Meyerstein that you are moved as soon as we can do so in a controlled way. Do you understand?"

"I ain't going anywhere, man."

"Not an option, Kathleen. You either cooperate and do as you're told and get in the trunk of a car unseen, or you will be bundled into a car in the next five minutes and driven out of there. So you either play nice or you get a rough ride. You choose."

Burke felt tears spill down her face. "What the fuck ... what the fuck is happening?"

"It is what it is. Do you understand?"

"I'm not getting in any fucking trunk. I'm claustrophobic. Do you understand?"

"We can get you sedated."

Burke felt helpless. "Jon, can I say something?"

"Sure, what's on your mind?"

"I'm scared ... I'm real scared now."

"Kathleen, now listen to me. That's natural. Don't be ashamed to be scared. We all get scared."

"What about you?"

"What about me?"

"You didn't look like the sort of guy that would get scared. You must think I'm stupid."

"Kathleen, you need to focus and pull yourself together. The Feds will get you out of there in an unmarked car. But you need to get in the trunk, and we can get you to a safe house."

Burke dabbed her eyes. "I can't do that."

"Can't do what?"

"I can't get in a fucking trunk. So that's it. I just want to go now!"

Burke ended the call and handed the phone to the Fed. "Let's get the fuck out of here, why don't we?"

TWENTY-FIVE

Matt Pearce snorted a line of coke off the back of his hand using a rolled-up twenty- dollar bill as he sat in his car, concealed in an alley in sight of the front of the house. He felt the rush washing through his body. He felt euphoric. The drug was touching his senses. He felt invincible.

He stared down the dirt road, partially concealed by palm trees and on-street parked cars. The post- man's outfit was in the trunk of his car. And he was seriously considering whether it would be needed, as there was no sign of the target.

Pearce had to get this right. If not, his brother would be next. It was the way it was. It was brutal. But effective. He felt a secondary wave through his body as the blood rushed through his veins and arteries to his brain. The high was indescribable. He felt aroused.

He didn't care now if time dragged. It took how- ever long it took.

Pearce had been told by his brother that the Feds would be protecting her. He assumed there would be two, maybe three inside the property with Burke.

He knew this would be a tricky one. His usual modus operandi was a knife to the neck. Quick, silent and deadly. He didn't mind staring into some fuck's eyes as they gasped their last breath.

In the distance an SUV turned into the street and pulled up outside the house.

Pearce's heart began to race. His watching and waiting had paid off. He sniffed hard and felt the last residue of the coke shoot straight to his brain. He was wired. Then three guys in suits came into view. It was the Feds flanking a small woman wearing shades and a Panama hat. She slid into the back seat, one Fed either side. The third Fed sat in the passenger seat up front.

The car pulled away.

Pearce started up the car and pulled away. He knew exactly what he was going to do.

TWENTY-SIX

Meyerstein was pacing the room, cellphone pressed to her ear, waiting for the Miami Fed to answer.

"Special Agent O'Halloran, ma'am. How can I help?" His voice was measured and calm.

"What the hell is going on?"

"Ma'am?"

"Why didn't you stop Kathleen Burke leaving the house in such a manner?"

"Ma'am, she's a goddamn law unto herself. I made the decision to just go with it, get her out of the house, and take it from there."

Meyerstein sighed. "Where exactly are you?"

"Ma'am, we're headed into Pensacola. We've got a perfect place lined up for her."

"Goddamn."

"Ma'am, I thought it was important to get the subject out asap."

"Unfortunately, a more controlled low-key exit might have been better. We could have had a decoy car or two – you know the drill."

"Ma'am, we've got an ETA of six minutes and we're fine."

"O'Halloran, is she with you just now?"

"Yeah, you want to talk?"

"Put her on."

A woman coughing. "Yeah, Meyerstein, what is it now?"

Meyerstein bristled at Burke's arrogance. She wondered if she should give her a ticking-off for not following instructions. But that was difficult if the special agent in charge was going to allow her to walk all over him. "Just to let you know you'll be in a nice new place in a few minutes."

Silence down the line.

"Are you still there, Kathleen?"

"Yeah, I'm here. Just freaked out to find that fuck's been tracking me for years. He must've known I was hanging out at the Outlaws club-house."

"Well, that's in the past. Let's start looking forward to a new future."

"Oh yeah, that's easy for you to say. You don't have to live in fear of Hunter and his crew."

"You're safe from them now."

"I don't feel very safe."

A loud bang like a car backfiring.

"What was that, Kathleen?"

"Think we've got a blowout."

"You kidding me?"

"Hang on … we're slowing down. The right rear has blown out. Fuck."

Meyerstein shook her head and snapped her

fingers to get Reznick's attention. "Jon, they've got a blowout."

Reznick grabbed the phone off her. "Who's this?"

"It's Kathleen."

"Kathleen, now listen to me. Get on the floor. And tell your driver not to slow down. I repeat, do not slow down."

"They're pulling over."

"No! Put the Fed on the line!"

A brief pause. "Special Agent O'Halloran speaking."

"This is Jon Reznick, working with Assistant Director Meyerstein. What the fuck is going on?"

"Relax, just a blowout."

"Have you pulled over?"

"Yeah, our driver is having a look."

"Get the fuck out of there! Do not stop!"

"What are you talking about?" A silence opened up for a few moments. "Shit."

"What is it?"

"Hold on … I've just got out the car to have a look. The tire's been shot out. High-powered rifle by the look of it."

Reznick felt sick. "O'Halloran, get your ass out of there. Do you understand?"

Then the line went dead.

TWENTY-SEVEN

Kathleen Burke was sitting in the back of the SUV, a Fed beside her on the phone, two of the Feds outside. "I thought O'Halloran was getting me to a new place. We're stuck in some shithole in Pensacola. This is bullshit."

The Fed beside her held up his finger as if she should be quiet. "Yeah, we need a back-up vehicle right away. And a tow truck. Seemingly there's no spare tire. No idea why."

Burke shook her head. "Un-be-fucking-lievable. You don't have a spare set of wheels? You're the FBI for chrissakes. Are you kidding me?"

The Fed ended the call. "You mind?"

"Look, I heard O'Halloran. Someone shot out the tire."

"We don't know. It looks like that."

"So how long do I have to wait?"

"Help's on the way. A matter of minutes. It's a priority."

"I don't like this. I'm scared."

"Kathleen, take a deep breath and get yourself under control."

Burke closed her eyes. Was it a warning? Or was it a signal they were about to kill her?

TWENTY-EIGHT

Matt Pearce parked up just over a block away after taking the long-range shot on the move. He adjusted the stolen Pensacola police badge round his neck He couldn't help the grin on his face. He felt on fire.

He was wearing a denim shirt to cover up his jailhouse tattoos, jeans, sneakers and a Dolphins hat and shades. He got out of the car and walked the block toward the SUV with its lights flashing, two suits standing outside, one talking into a cellphone.

Pearce walked up to the Fed on the phone. "Just passing. Can I give you guys a hand?"

The Fed smiled, covered the phone with his hand. "Thanks all the same, officer." He flashed his badge. "FBI. We got this."

"You got a flat?"

"I said we got this, officer. Thank you very much."

Pearce smiled and pulled the 9mm out from the back of his jeans and pressed it against the Fed's head. He fired once and the blood and brain matter exploded onto the side of the car. He spun round, shot the other Fed point-blank. Then he trained the gun on the Fed inside and blew his brains out.

He opened the rear passenger door.

Time seemed to have slowed down.

Inside, cowering on the floor, was Kathleen Burke, hands trying to shield her face.

"Please! Please! I have a son!"

Pearce aimed the gun at Burke's head and smiled. "Hunter says hi." He fired two shots to the back of her head, blood and brain splattering across the leather seats and the windows.

He turned and walked away, warm blood dripping off his face.

TWENTY-NINE

Hunter Cain was dripping in sweat as he pummeled a punching bag in the basement gym of the ocean-front property on Fisher Island, Miami. Upstairs, behind closed drapes, were his two comrades, willing to spill blood and give their lives for what they believed in. But he sensed a growing tension as the hour grew closer.

Cain punched hard with a right and then a left. And then a right. And then a left. Then he did some free weights for half an hour. Then the medicine ball. He pounded the treadmill, clocking up the miles, headphones on. Metallica blaring out loud. He felt the endorphins kicking in.

When Cain was finished, he showered and put on fresh clothes provided by the ex-military instructor who rented the property. It was a tight crew. The way he liked it. He knew each and every one of them.

He went up to the lounge area where Pearce was watching Fox.

"Hey, check this out, Hunter," he said.

A blonde TV reporter was standing in front a

taped-off police crime scene, a car with its doors opened, partially screened from onlookers. "Sources within the FBI have confirmed that three special agents have been shot dead, along with a woman who has not been formally identified. Speculation has mounted that the woman was the target of a gangland assassination."

Cain stared at the TV and looked at Pearce. "Holy fuck."

A cellphone begin to ring. Pearce answered. "Yeah, bro, talk to me." He nodded and looked at Cain. "You want to speak to him?" A nod. Pearce handed him the phone. "Hunter, my brother."

Cain gathered his thoughts as he stared at the TV image of the car. "Matt, what the fuck were you playing at?"

"Hunter, you asked me to take care of it."

"You dumb fuck. I wanted her dead. Why didn't you just kneecap the Feds?"

A long sigh. "Hunter … sorry, I don't understand, man. I thought you wanted it dealt with?"

"I wanted it dealt with. You know what this is? This is ratcheting things up a notch or ten. Do you understand the heat that we're going to get for this? Bad enough the jailbreak, but they're going to dump this right back at my door now. And I'm telling you, man, I ain't too happy about how you've handled this."

"Hunter, man, what can I say? I thought I was following orders."

"Since when did I say kill three Feds, you dumb fuck?"

"What do you want me to do?"

Hunter ran a hand through his hair. "You disappear, okay?"

"Got it."

"No usual haunts. I mean *really* disappear."

"Mexico?"

"Definitely not Mexico. They'll have the borders sealed up real good."

"Montana?"

"Montana is good. Wyoming is good. Just keep out of sight, and disappear. And keep your mouth shut."

"Hunter, man, I didn't realize it was going to go down like that."

Cain sighed. "What's done is done. The main thing is, she's gone. But you need to get out of sight for the next two years. Maybe more."

The line went dead.

THIRTY

Meyerstein was hooked up to a videoconference screen within Miami-Dade police HQ, her boss on the big screen staring down at her.

"Martha, with immediate effect I'm relieving you of your duties. Do you understand?"

"Sir, with all due respect, I'm not going to comply with that instruction."

"Do you want me to fire you for insubordination?"

"Sir, I'm asking you to listen to me."

"There's nothing to talk about. This is a terrible day for the Bureau. This is a fuck-up. Three special agents killed and a witness all gunned down. I'm appalled."

"So am I, sir."

"Martha, this happened on your watch!"

"Sir, with all due respect, that's bullshit. The special agent should have stopped Kathleen Burke before she left the safe house. She should have been restrained if need be. But as it was, he ignored Jon Reznick's instructions to wait till there were two other cars to screen the getaway and act as a decoy."

"What?"

"Sir, Kathleen Burke effectively just got up and stormed out of the house, and the two Feds just went along with it. Now I'm not pointing the finger. God rest their souls, they're good men. But you know as well as I do, sir, that they should have secured the area, namely, the unpredictable Kathleen Burke, before they headed off. In effect they allowed her to bully them."

O'Donoghue rubbed his eyes and let out a long sigh. "This doesn't take away from the fact that you have already disobeyed an instruction and allowed Jon Reznick to continue with this investigation."

"Sir, this is getting us nowhere. This Jon Reznick fixation does not address the failings of these two relatively inexperienced special agents. It most certainly would not have happened in Miami, for example."

"Martha, you're going to give me no choice. If you don't accept this suspension, I will fire your ass out of the FBI. Now I don't want to do it, you know that. But I can't have this insubordination and recklessness."

"Jon Reznick gave excellent advice to Kathleen Burke to stay put, and for two cars to be part of the operation to get her out of there. I also wanted to get her in the trunk, but she started going crazy, talking about being claustrophobic. The fact of the matter is that this terrible chain of events is the work of Hunter Cain."

"The guy that escaped?"

"This is his payback."

"Hang on, Martha. From what I heard, the actions of Jon Reznick may have sparked this."

Meyerstein gathered her thoughts. "Sir, I think to point the finger at Jon Reznick as being in some way culpable because of his getting in a few Hell's Angels' faces at a clubhouse is really stretching things to breaking point."

"Martha, I'm at breaking point. So should you be."

"Sir, she was taken into safe custody. She was under the protection of the FBI. We fucked up, not Jon Reznick. It is just plain wrong to say we should have foreseen that Cain would send a tracking device within a silver cross. We are dealing with a very, very dangerous man. Who will stop at nothing. And deploy Aryan Brotherhood lone wolves to carry out whatever he wants. Sir, you don't want to fire my ass. And I don't want you to fire my ass. We need to catch Hunter Cain. And you know why?"

"You think he'll still be planning a spectacular? After today?"

"Hunter Cain will stop at nothing."

The director took a few moments to speak. "I've told the director of Homeland Security I was going to suspend you. He's going to wonder who's in charge of the FBI."

"Sir, I've been on this for days since the breakout. Jon Reznick knows Hunter Cain better than anyone.

If you want recriminations, suspensions and firings, fine, but not now. We're all on the same side. Now is not the time for rash decisions. And I will make this promise, sir. I will find Hunter Cain, and I will bring him in, dead or alive. But I need Jon Reznick on this."

The director stared down at her for what seemed like a lifetime. "I need to know something."

"Yes, sir."

"I need to know if you think we can locate this Cain and apprehend him in time."

"Sir, if he's anything like Reznick says he is, this is not going to end well."

"Very well. I'm not going to place any obstacles in your way. But I want Reznick to be on a far tighter leash, you understand me?"

"Yes, sir."

"Move with immediate effect to Miami FBI field office. I'll message them myself."

"Thank you, sir. Appreciate that. What about Homeland Security?"

"What about them?"

"What will they say?"

"Let me worry about them. Your job is simple: find Cain and neutralize this fucker. Do you understand?"

THIRTY-ONE

"What a fucking mess," Reznick said, as he sat around a conference table at the FBI's Miami field office as Meyerstein, Stamper and a dozen other counter-terrorism experts mulled over the sequence of events. He sipped some scalding-hot black coffee as they talked of scenarios and targets for Cain.

Reznick pushed his coffee aside, stood up and began to pace the room. He kicked over a trash can full of shredded paper. "Motherfucker!"

The room went quiet at Reznick's outburst.

Special Agent Gillian Miller, who Reznick had met in DC, blushed. She cleared her throat. "So where does that leave us? Whatever is going to happen is going to go down in or around Miami. It narrows it down."

Reznick looked at the faces around the table. "I mentioned previously about Hunter Cain's obsession with Timothy McVeigh. Would the actions of this sidekick of his, gunning down three special agents, indicate that's where they're coming from?"

"I think it would indicate firstly how ruthless they are, clearly. But, yes, absolutely, it shows that

Cain and his crew or terrorist cell, call it what you will, don't give a damn for the lives of federal officers. McVeigh, as you'll all know, had that same pathological hatred of government."

Meyerstein leaned back in her seat. "Let's leave all that to one side. I'm fairly certain we can say that Cain is a right-wing militia leader, and perhaps he's in the same mold as McVeigh, with his military training. My problem is, where is he? So far, NSA has got nothing."

Reznick nodded. "Which probably not only indicates that Cain is smart enough to change phones every day, maybe more than once a day, but also points to a network. A crew of people who are backing, supporting and helping Cain and these guys. People behind the scenes." He looked over at Miller. "I know Hunter Cain well. I was in Delta alongside him. He's a tough, tough fuck. Clearly off the scale now. But he's not stupid. The killing of these three Feds would have annoyed him. He might not give a damn for the lives lost. But he'd be mightily pissed off that the mission he's on, whatever it is, would attract attention from us. It's one thing to kill his ex-girlfriend in FBI custody, which is a pretty unbelievable screw-up in the first place. But I was trained the same as him. The mission is everything. The mission is sacrosanct."

Stamper looked up from his notes and glowered across at Reznick. "Jon, I don't like you talking about screw-ups. Three FBI men died. And I don't think this is the time or place to start pointing the finger of blame at colleagues of mine who have just been killed."

"Roy, you wanna just move on? We need to focus on bringing down Cain and stopping whatever it is he's planning."

Stamper looked across at Meyerstein. "I don't like him sitting in on meetings."

Meyerstein leaned forward, hands clasped. "Too bad, Roy. Now, Gillian, I want the latest analysis on what's happening."

Special Agent Miller cleared her throat and took a drink of water. "Hunter Cain had a vast library in his cell. Hundreds of books piled up. Half of them were about Timothy McVeigh. Initially we were thinking it might be the start of an inter-militia war on control of meth dealing in Florida. But the current thinking seems to be that something big might very well be underway. There are currently four major events in town. A social media conference, a sci-fi convention, an Apple conference and a fund-raising gala for Syrian refugees."

Reznick sighed. "There's nothing else happening in Miami?"

Meyerstein said, "Exactly what kind of things had you in mind, Jon?"

"G7 conference, security summit, Nato conference, intra-government type thing."

Miller shrugged. "Nothing like that in Miami or Florida over the next year. There's a visit by the president, but that's penciled in by the Secret Service for next March."

Reznick began to pace the room one more time. "I don't get it. I just don't get it. He's been sprung – and make no mistake he has been sprung – to carry out a big job. I don't believe he would have been sprung to take out a Hell's Angel, a meth dealer or some liberal senator. McVeigh attacked a federal building. Now I'm not saying that's the target. But what I'm saying is that this is going to be big. Major. What does Cain know? He understands guns, rifles, tactical awareness, and it makes him a natural leader. If he wanted to kill a rival, he wouldn't fuck around. He would just go, watch him, and kill him as soon as he could."

Meyerstein threw down her pen. "Goddamn it, when are we going to get a break?"

Everyone around the table just stared at her but said nothing.

THIRTY-TWO

Hunter Cain pinned up a map of Fisher Island on the plasterboard wall of the basement of the Fisher Island house as Ken Pearce and Neil Foley sat, arms crossed. He made a black cross with a marker pen. "We are here." Then he pointed to a location at the other side of the island. "This is where it's going to go down."

Pearce nodded but Foley said nothing.

"Like most operations, surprise is the best calling card. They won't be expecting us. Why? Because we're going to gain entry with uniforms worn only by staff inside the complex. Made to measure. And don't worry – the outfits will cover the tats, okay?"

Foley stared at the map and sighed. "Hunter, can I be honest, man?"

Cain shrugged. "Of course. What's on your mind, bro?"

"The objectives of the mission. They seem kinda blurry to me."

Cain was surprised at Foley's cooler tone. "Blurry? I'm sorry, I don't follow."

"Don't get me wrong, this is gonna be something

unbelievable, but I'm wondering, what exactly will it achieve? I mean … I'm not too sure this has been really thought through. Just my take on it."

Cain nodded. He felt a rage burning within him. He couldn't abide indecision and people going cold on a plan. He liked decisiveness. "Well, okay, firstly, this *has* been thought through. By myself and others. And the objectives are pretty basic. Fundamental stuff. And there are going to be casualties. Any war has casualties, and inevitably there will be innocents who lose their lives. That's just the way it is. It's the way it's always been."

Foley sighed and scratched the back of his head. "Don't get me wrong, Hunter, I've got no problem about shedding blood. You know that."

Cain stared at Foley. He felt as if a switch had been flicked in his head.

"But … I don't know … it all seems very sketchy, the objectives. I'm not feeling it."

Cain cleared his throat. "Not feeling it." He took a deep breath and sighed. "Are you fucking kidding me?"

"I just want to know."

Cain's stomach knotted. "It's about reclaiming our country back from the billionaires, the lobbyists, the corporations and the corrupt politicians. But it's also a call to arms. We're firing the starting gun in what we hope is an uprising. And, yeah, it'll get messy. Ultimately this is about a second American revolution. Cleaning out the shit.

Shocking ordinary Americans out of their lethargy. But it's also about starting again. Starting clean."

Pearce nodded, eyes glistening. "Absolutely."

Cain took a step towards Foley. "What we don't want is for the small guy, the ordinary Joe, to be downtrodden any longer in his own country. We want our country back. And we're prepared to die doing so. Do you understand now?"

Foley opened the palms of his hands as if still not getting it. "Here's the thing. While I absolutely agree with taking the fight to these fuckers, my question is, is this the right place and time to do it?"

Cain went quiet for a few moments. "Neil, I'm going to be very straight with you, bro. I love you, man. But I want you to be straight with me. Do you understand?"

Foley nodded. "Sure, can't argue with that, man."

"Neil, do you want out, is that it?"

Foley blew out his cheeks. "I don't know."

"You getting cold feet, is that it?"

"Yeah … I guess I am."

Cain said nothing.

Foley shrugged. "Sorry, bro, I gotta be out. I got a family. I need to think of stuff like that."

Cain stood and stared at Foley for a few moments. He stepped forward and reached out to shake Foley's hand. The grip was tight. Then they hugged. "No hard feelings, bro. I admire your honesty."

Foley turned and hugged Pearce.

Whilst Foley's back was turned, Cain reached into his boots and pulled out a knife. He lunged forward and thrust it hard into Foley's lower back three times. Blood spilled out of Foley's shirt, pooling on the marble floor. He groaned and fell to his knees.

Foley looked up, eyes pleading, bleeding out everywhere.

Cain kneeled down. He grabbed Foley by the hair and stabbed him again and again in the chest. He must have stabbed him thirty, maybe forty times. He was drenched in Foley's blood. He got to his feet and spat on Foley's lifeless body. He turned and stared at Pearce, who was as impassive as ever. "It is what it is, right?"

"Fucker crossed the line, Hunter. You had no choice, man."

"Exactly. Let's get this cleared up and get the fuck out of here."

THIRTY-THREE

It was a fifteen-minute recess and Reznick was pacing a windowless conference room in the FBI's Miami field office as Meyerstein flicked through some briefing notes. He shook his head and looked around at the empty chairs. "Meyerstein, we're missing something. Something doesn't add up."

Meyerstein leaned back in her seat and shrugged. "What doesn't add up? We have the best minds from all the counter-terrorism and intelligence agencies working together in this joint terrorism task force. We're giving it everything we've got. You know what's missing?"

Reznick shook his head. "I do know something feels not quite right."

"I don't believe that kind of thinking is getting us anywhere."

"Yeah, but don't you see? No one is asking fundamental questions about how the hell we've got so many agents working on this case, and yet we still can't find the fucker, and also don't know what the hell the target is. This just doesn't make sense to me."

"We're all working very hard, Jon, as you know, to get to these guys. It's just a matter of time."

"Meyerstein, let's step back from this and look at what we have."

"Jon, please don't patronize me."

"I'm not patronizing you. I want to talk about this. We need to get back to basics. We seem to have gotten lost in a world of hypothetical scenarios and analysis."

"I don't disagree with what you're saying so far."

"Meyerstein, what are we all agreed on?"

"We all agree that Hunter Cain is with two Aryan Brotherhood enforcers and they're planning something major."

Reznick clicked his fingers. "Bingo! Absolutely. Something major."

"I'm sorry – I don't follow."

"What three things are on just now in or around Miami? What did Agent Miller say? A social media conference, a sci-fi convention, an Apple conference and a fundraising gala for Syrian refugees."

"You're not suggesting any of these would be the target?"

"No, I'm not. Which leads me to my point. What are we missing?"

"Missing? I'm sorry – I don't follow."

"There are no would-be spectaculars that come to mind if we're thinking right-wing militias."

Meyerstein sighed. "At a push, the fundraising gala for Syrian refuges may be something they'd object to, although I don't hold that view myself."

"Forget fundraising galas. Hunter Cain is after big fish. He's been sprung to do something big in Miami, would you agree?"

Meyerstein lifted up her pen and pointed at a map of South Florida on the wall. "Well, either Miami or South Florida."

"Right. So why the hell isn't there something that comes to mind?"

"Look Jon, we've checked and double-checked this: these events are the only places where there will be either significant numbers or that are big convention-type events which would lend themselves to a spectacular."

"Agent Miller – she gave us this list?"

"Agent Miller is one of our finest agents, Jon. Please don't cast aspersions on her competence."

"No one's casting aspersions. What if the information she had to hand was all the information the FBI were aware of?"

"Jon, I'm sorry to be acting dumb on this, but what the hell are you getting at?"

"Have you considered a scenario whereby because of the sensitive nature of a gathering, perhaps security concerns, the FBI hasn't been in on something? Is that a possibility?"

"Jon, I think you're reaching."

"Why are there no realistic targets that might interest such a group of right-wing patriots?"

Meyerstein went quiet for a few moments, as if

mulling over what he'd said. "Let me get this straight. Do you think that, because we're framing this around what we know is going on, we might be limiting ourselves, as we don't know exactly what's going on?"

"Let me spell it out to you. What if, and it is a big if, the FBI is not in the loop regarding a gathering in Miami that has security implications?"

"That's impossible."

"Impossible, or highly unlikely?"

"Impossible. We know what's going on?"

"What if there are agencies that are not sharing what they know? Inter-agency rivalries, turf wars, and all that?"

"Jon, that's in the past. That doesn't happen. Trust me, we work together."

Reznick sat down in his seat and looked across the table at her. "Meyerstein, we need to go the extra mile. We make assumptions. Details that should be passed to another agency somehow aren't. It happens, right?"

"Jon, I'm not buying this."

"I'm not asking you to buy it. I'm asking you to get Agent Miller and her team to go back and reach out individually to intelligence agencies, and find out if there's anything in Miami we need to know about, or if there are sensitive meetings we don't know about."

"Look, if there's anything major, we're always the first agency in the loop."

"Let's go that extra mile. What harm will it do?"

"It might be wasting precious time."

A few Feds started filing back into the room. "Let's triple-check this, why don't we?"

THIRTY-FOUR

Just after midnight, Hunter Cain and Pearce were picked up from the underground parking garage of the property by the military man coordinating things. He pulled away in his Jeep Renegade through the huge electronic steel gates, and down a wide palm-fringed street. "Just so you know, guys, Foley has been disposed of."

Cain was sitting up front. "Needs must. The operation comes first, right?"

The man nodded. "Fucking A."

Cain said, "Okay, so how long till the destination?"

"ETA eight minutes."

"But they'll be choppered in, right?"

"Absolutely. Reduced things massively. But it does leave them vulnerable to those on the inside."

Cain grinned. "Motherfuckers." He turned and looked round at Pearce, who patted him on the shoulder. "They're going to pay. We're going to light this fire. And, make no mistake, people are gonna get hurt."

Pearce nodded. "How long now?"

Cain turned and faced the driver. "Not long now, right?"

"You're on the home straight. This is just to give you a feel for the road, and intersections and such-like."

Cain said, "What about police patrols?"

"It's all perimeter and inside. Nothing at all out in the community. Nobody knows this is going on. How cool is that?"

Cain began to laugh. "Motherfuckers!"

THIRTY-FIVE

The early-morning sun was peeking through the fronds of the palm trees as Meyerstein paced the parking lot of the FBI in North Miami Beach, coffee in hand. With her was Jon Reznick, leaning against an SUV.

"Jon," she said, "everyone in that goddamn room is busting their ass on this, so give me a break, will you?"

Reznick turned and sat down on some steps. "We're missing something. There's a piece of the jigsaw not in place."

"You keep on saying that, Jon, but we've gone over everything, and we're drawing a blank."

Special Agent Gillian Miller stepped out and approached Meyerstein. She looked ashen-faced. "Ma'am, we got a problem."

"Yeah, tell me about it."

"I've been reaching out to all the agencies, one by one."

"And?"

"Ma'am, I have two systems experts on my team …"

"I know, I recruited them myself."

"They spotted a discrepancy, just over fifteen minutes ago."

"What kind of discrepancy?"

"They're still doing some tests, but they're near as dammit certain – three messages sent to three separate individuals at the FBI in Florida have been intercepted by a third party."

Meyerstein stared at Special Agent Miller, who began to flush under the harsh gaze. "Who intercepted them, and why?"

"We believe the IP address is being spoofed, so we can't track it down. Pretty sophisticated operation."

"What else?"

Miller cleared her throat as Reznick approached her. "Am I good to continue?"

"Jon has full security clearance, Agent Miller."

Miller nodded. "Here's the kicker. The three encrypted messages were sent from the Secret Service to the FBI, alerting us that a sensitive conference would be held in the city."

Meyerstein ran a hand through her hair. "Jesus Christ, what the hell? So the FBI in Miami is unaware of something about to happen, is that what you're saying?"

"We're not leading on this."

"So what's happening?"

"Just over a month ago, the private security company responsible for this conference changed the location, which was in upstate New York, alerting the Secret Service as to why."

"What's the conference?"

Miller blew out her cheeks. "It's a planning meeting ahead of a major Bilderberg conference."

"You're kidding me."

Miller shook her head. "The security head of Secure Solutions Inc. got information about credible threats from anarchist groups and far-left-wing groups in New York trying to disrupt the conference."

"And they decided to move it down to Miami?"

Miller nodded. "A former president is scheduled to speak at this planning meeting, talking about what goes on the agenda. That's where the Secret Service come into this."

"What about Miami-Dade police?"

"Just checked with them. They know nothing either. We're working on the assumption that those who have compromised the FBI's system have done the same for Miami-Dade police."

Reznick nodded. "So it's a strategy meeting organized by the Bilderberg Group. We're talking wealthy corporate, military and political interests."

Miller looked at the list. "Goldman Sachs, Bank of America, IMF, a smattering of industrialists from Europe. They're all part of the pre-planning group."

Reznick said, "Where exactly is this?"

"A luxury hotel on Fisher Island."

Meyerstein stared at Reznick; then she fixed her gaze on Miller. "Get the FBI director on the phone right this minute. And get a chopper ready. I've heard enough."

THIRTY-SIX

Hunter Cain checked himself in the full-length mirror of a bedroom in the waterfront home. He wore a navy suit, white shirt with pale-blue silk tie, and black shoes polished to a deep shine. He picked up the lanyard with his fake FBI photo ID and hung it around his neck. He turned to look at Pearce, who was buttoning his shirt. "How you feeling?"

Pearce's eyes were glazed as if he was in the zone. "I'm good. Real good. Whatever goes down today, bro, I just want to say I love you, man."

Cain hugged Pearce tight. "Today, we're going to go down in history. We're going to light this fucking touchpaper. We're patriots. And we're taking our country back."

Pearce grinned. "Fucking A."

The pair headed downstairs where the ex-military instructor was waiting, also wearing a smart dark suit, white shirt, dark-red tie and shiny black shoes. "Us white boys scrub up well, what do you say?"

Cain grinned and hugged the instructor. "Let's get it on."

They headed down to the underground parking garage. Cain sat up front, Pearce in the back, as the instructor got behind the wheel. He started the car and the garage door opened.

They pulled away and headed in the direction of the luxury resort. The men sat in silence with their own thoughts. Fears.

Cain cranked up the air con a notch. The cool air felt good. A few minutes later, they caught sight of an outer security cordon. They pulled up.

The instructor flashed his badge. "Morning. FBI."

The security guard used a handheld reader to scan the ID badge of the driver. Then he scanned the badges of Cain and Pearce. "Thank you, gentlemen." He turned and pointed in the direction of a huge parking lot adjacent to the complex.

They were ushered through a secondary security cordon.

A huge security guard, holding an iPad with a list of names, nodded. "They're good."

Cain and the two others walked a couple of hundred yards to a third screen zone where they were photographed and their biometrics checked with their records.

The female guard gave a thumbs-up to her colleague, who was running a security wand over the three men. "They're good."

The man nodded and stepped back. "Welcome, gentlemen," he said, pointing to the side entrance of the huge hotel complex. "The delegates will be arriving in the next couple of hours. If you need anything, don't hesitate to let us know."

Cain smiled. "Much appreciated."

He turned, the other two close behind, and headed inside.

THIRTY-SEVEN

Jon Reznick stared out of the window as he sat beside Meyerstein in the back of an FBI chopper headed for Fisher Island. She glanced at the iPad on her lap as another message came in from Stamper. He adjusted his headset and mouthpiece, and turned to face her. "Meyerstein, can you hear me?"

Meyerstein nodded. "Sure, Jon. What's on your mind?"

"Let's talk about logistics. How many agents have we got working this?"

"More than a hundred as we speak. Two FBI SWAT teams are being scrambled."

"ETA for them?"

"They're loading up now. Assume they'll be at least ten minutes behind us. We've also got two six-man teams headed on a boat direct to Fisher Island."

Reznick nodded, glad she was covering all bases.

Meyerstein replied to Stamper's message and looked again at Reznick. "I'm worried."

"Not surprised."

"No … I'm worried I might be overreacting. We

have no proof Cain or anyone is there or will be there, or is even aware this is going on."

"Do you really think that?"

Meyerstein sighed and shook her head. "I don't know. These miscommunications happen. Inter-agency failings et cetera."

"Meyerstein, listen to me. This fits the bill perfectly. Ninety delegates, a sub-committee of the main body, meeting to discuss the agenda for a major Bilderberg conference in the fall. This is low-key. No media invited. No one knows about it. It's not the main thing to attract serious attention from the mainstream media."

The chopper dipped as they hit turbulence over Biscayne Bay.

Meyerstein cleared her throat as she regained her composure, and looked at the pilot. "We okay?"

The pilot turned and nodded. "Yes, ma'am. Just crosswinds. We're fine. We're having to take a different route from what I'd usually do."

"What do you mean?"

The pilot went quiet for a few moments. "Sorry, ma'am. Roy Stamper is on the line. You want to speak to him?"

"Sure, put him on."

The headset crackled as Stamper's voice came on the headset. "Martha, airspace from the airport to the resort on Fisher Island is blocked off."

"What the hell are you talking about, Roy?"

"Martha, I've just spoken to the Secret Service.

And they're confirming that as a former president is among the delegates and guests, they're not allowing choppers anywhere near this air channel."

"Roy, that's bullshit."

"They're pulling rank on it."

"Did you tell them what we're facing?"

"They're adamant."

"So what the hell are we supposed to do?"

"We've got a car ready for you and Jon at the playing fields on the opposite side of the island. It's inconvenient, I know. But it is what it is."

Meyerstein turned and faced Reznick. "Jon, did you get that?"

Reznick shrugged. "Let's roll with it. We land. We move on."

Meyerstein ended the call. The chopper banked low as it turned and headed for Fisher Island. In the distance, Reznick caught the first sight of storm clouds rolling into the bay.

THIRTY-EIGHT

Hunter Cain pressed the earpiece in tight as he got his bearings and headed down a stairwell. He lifted the cuff of his jacket sleeve to his face. "Can you give me your bearings?"

His earpiece buzzed into life. "Fifteen yards behind you, sir," Pearce said.

"Number three?"

The voice of the instructor. "Walking the corridors as we speak, making sure we're all clear. I repeat. We are all clear. The auditorium is filling up. Delegates have arrived. Airspace still closed off for twenty minutes around complex. And we are good. Inspection proceeding."

Cain's heart began to beat harder as he descended the stairs. Deeper and deeper into the bowels of the complex. He went through a No Entry door and headed further down. Along a concrete tunnel, past a boiler room and then through another door to a locker room in a sub-basement. "I'm in the locker room. Have you got this covered?"

Pearce coughed hard. "Yes, sir, we are in the

adjacent room. No one is coming in or out. And we're good to go on this."

Cain strode down the rows of gun-metal gray lockers till he came to locker 2301. It was locked. He pulled out a key and opened it up. He peered in. Empty inside. He reached in and pressed his hand to the back of the locker and felt for a tiny switch in a metal crevice. He flicked it and pulled away the false rear of the locker. Behind that was a brown leather briefcase. He pulled it out and unzipped the bag. Inside was a Semtex suicide vest, fake beard, horn-rimmed spectacles, a new ID lanyard, steel handcuffs and a 9mm Glock.

Cain strapped on the Semtex vest and pressed a switch activating the device. He put on the fake beard and horn-rimmed spectacles and hung the ID lanyard round his neck. Then he zipped up the brief-case and walked out of the locker room. He walked past Pearce, his blocker.

His earpiece buzzed into life. "Auditorium filling up for the first session," said the instructor. "Are you on your way?"

"Two minutes. Don't start without us."

THIRTY-NINE

Meyerstein's car pulled up at the outer security cordon and she stepped out. She walked up to the huge security guard, Reznick by her side, and flashed her badge. "FBI," she said. "Assistant Director Meyerstein. Who is your head of security?"

The man-mountain shrugged. "Your guys are already inside."

"What are you talking about?"

"Three Feds, Miami FBI."

"Get me your head of security now, goddamit!"

The man radioed the instruction. A few moments later a well-groomed man in a pale-blue suit appeared.

"Trevor Armstrong," he said. "How can I help?"

Meyerstein sighed and repeated what she had said to the security guard. "So we need immediate access. I also want to see the details of the FBI individuals who went through earlier."

"I'm sorry – that's not possible. This area is out of your jurisdiction. We run a very tight ship. And whilst I'd be delighted to grant you extra passes, it might take an hour or so."

Meyerstein took a step forward and stared at the man. "Maybe I didn't make myself clear. We need to know who is here today. Now."

"The database is strictly confidential. You can understand that."

The sound of a car pulling up sharply could be heard behind them. Meyerstein turned and saw it was full of FBI Miami. She signaled the special agent in charge across. "Jimmy, come here," she said.

Jimmy Albright stepped forward and stood beside Meyerstein. "Ma'am?"

"This gentleman says there are three accredited FBI Miami special agents already inside."

Albright screwed up his face. "Absolutely, categorically not."

Reznick stepped forward and eyeballed the head of security. "Categorically not, he said. So here's the thing, pal. You either move aside or you'll be placed under arrest. What's it going to be?"

The head of security showed his palms. "Woah … guys."

"Make the call," Reznick said, "right fucking now!"

The head of security said, "You can't have access to such things!"

Reznick grabbed the man by the throat and pressed tight. "This is how it's going to work, you sanctimonious fuck. We're going in. And you're going to stay here with your guys and make sure no one leaves."

The man's eyes were filling with tears. "Sure, sure!" He handed an iPad with a list of delegates and security attendees to Reznick.

Reznick let the man go and began to scan the list as Meyerstein edged closer.

"Jon, we really need to work on your social skills."

"Let's talk about that later." He pulled up the names and photos of the three FBI accredited agents. Reznick immediately saw the unmistakable face of Hunter Cain and Ken Pearce. "These are our guys. And one other we don't know."

Meyerstein looked at the faces long and hard before she handed the iPad to Albright. "These your guys?"

"Absolutely not."

"I want full tactical back-up right now. This is a Code 42. Do you understand? And I want this place on total lockdown, got it?"

Albright nodded and pulled out his cellphone.

Reznick had seen enough. He brushed past the head of security. His men just looked on as Meyerstein followed close by.

"Jon, where are you going? You can't go in without a plan. You know that."

"It's too late for plans. We're clean out of time. Their operation is underway, Meyerstein. And we need to locate these fucks. This is going down as we speak."

FORTY

Hunter Cain squeezed into a spare seat in the back row of the main auditorium. He felt the contours of the Semtex plastic under his shirt. He grinned and adjusted his spectacles. Then he scratched the false beard under his chin. He turned and smiled at the delegates either side of him and they smiled back.

He turned and saw Pearce standing beside security, pretending to talk into his cellphone. His gaze wandered around the auditorium. At the far end, diagonally opposite where he was seated, he made eye contact with the instructor, who gave a small nod in his direction.

On the big screens a small bespectacled man appeared. Applause rang out. He walked on to the stage, a huge backdrop of the Manhattan skyline at night behind him.

Cain began to clap too. He nodded as those around joined in too. He felt a surge of adrenalin rush through him. He was so ready it was unreal.

The man on stage looked out over the audience and smiled. "Ladies and gentlemen, I'd like to welcome you all to this introductory meeting and greeting. We think it's never been so important to communicate and facilitate the exchange of ideas to protect and grow the economies of our world. Great cities like New York, where I live, know the importance of the global economy. The importance of strong security in an uncertain world. A more interconnected world. But a world where we need to defend our values."

Cain felt his stomach knot.

The man cleared his throat. "Our organization is much maligned. Some say it's a secretive club of bankers, politicians on the make, and military strategists who love starting wars. That's only partly true."

The auditorium erupted with laughter and clapping.

"But seriously, we are all about charting strategies for the twenty-first century and beyond. We've got to think even more seriously about existential threats. But also threats to the hegemony of the United States of America as the bulwark against China, a resurgent Russia and a recalcitrant Iran. We need to protect the interests of our America all around the world. And that's why, over the next forty-eight hours, we will hopefully come up with a working agenda for the Bilderberg conference in the fall."

Cain peered over the top of his glasses. He watched as the instructor got to his feet. Took out the Magnum. Fired two shots straight at the speaker's face. One side of the man's head ripped apart as blood and brains splattered onto the projected image of New York in the background. Screams and pandemonium as delegates ran for cover.

It was like in slow motion. The instructor turned and shot the man either side of him.

Cain stayed seated as everyone fled. The instructor shouted: "Freedom from tyranny!"

Then he put the gun in his mouth and blew his own brains out.

FORTY-ONE

The sound of the gunshots flicked a switch in Jon Reznick. He pushed his way through glass doors and headed in the direction of the gunfire. He turned and saw Meyerstein in hot pursuit, gun in hand. His earpiece crackled into life.

"Reznick." The voice of the special agent in charge of the FBI in Miami, Albright. "My guys are leading! Do you understand?"

"I don't see any SWAT. Listen, I'm on this. You need to tell me where Hunter Cain disappeared to once he was cleared to go inside."

"Jon, we're looking over the footage as we speak. He headed down to level minus three, which is a sub-basement, lockers."

"Then what?"

"He headed in with Pearce half a dozen yards behind him."

Reznick saw a sign for the auditorium. "He's the blocker. What else?"

"We can't see what's happened to him."

"No cameras inside?"

"Apparently not."

"Fuck. Listen, Albright, check the footage. Face recognition. Run it all. He's here."

"Will do. Take care."

The sound of screaming and shouting and arguing and frightened voices drifted towards him. Reznick headed through more doors and was met by a swarm of delegates rushing towards him, fleeing.

"Get the hell out of here, man!" one shouted at Reznick.

Reznick pressed on and pushed through the delegates. He turned and saw Meyerstein with a SWAT team.

"Jon, wait!" she shouted.

But Reznick didn't. He turned and headed into a lobby area, and then into the auditorium, the smell of gunshot and smoke in the air. He saw two men in suits bending down over the man on the podium, weeping. Reznick saw the man had been blown away at close range. But it wasn't Cain or Pearce. He turned and saw two security guards beside the shooter. Back of his head missing, oozing God knows what.

Reznick flashed his FBI badge. "There are two others!"

The guards just shrugged. "Man, I'm sorry. This is kinda fucked I guess, but I don't know what the hell is happening."

Reznick kicked over a chair and spoke into his cuff to confirm the shooter was dead. "Cain and

Pearce still inside the complex! The dead man is not Cain or Pearce!" He headed back out into the lobby. The earpiece crackled into life.

"Jon, we copy that. We just heard gunshots on the fourth floor."

Reznick headed through some doors to the stairwell and bounded up two steps at a time.

"SWAT are dealing with gunshots on the second floor. A dozen lying dead."

"Fuck."

"Please be aware Secret Service are on the fourth floor. They will shoot to kill."

"Good."

"One final thing."

"Hang on … standby."

Reznick headed up and up, heart pounding hard. He was only one level from the fourth. "What is it?"

"Cain is now wearing a beard and spectacles. He's shot two Secret Service men."

The line went dead.

Reznick had a sense of foreboding unlike any he'd ever known.

FORTY-TWO

Hunter Cain ignored the sound of screaming and alarms going off as he prowled the second floor. His earpiece crackled into life.

"Target identified on fourth floor." The voice of Pearce.

"Good work."

"Hunter, they got me. I'm not gonna make it, bro."

Cain felt as if his head was going to explode. "I'm coming, buddy." He rode the elevator to the fourth floor. He took out the handgun and concealed it behind his briefcase. The elevator door opened.

He could see Pearce lying soaked in blood and at a weird angle alongside two dead Secret Service agents.

Cain spotted the target in a state of shock stumbling past. He dropped the briefcase and grabbed him. Then he pressed the gun to the former president's temple.

Suddenly he saw another Secret Service man lying crouched on the corridor carpet, aiming a handgun in his direction.

"Put down the gun!" the guy shouted.

Cain pressed his face close to the back of the ex-president's ear. "How much you getting paid for taking blood money off the corporations, sir?"

The ex-president began to shake uncontrollably.

"What was that? You don't care? Is that what you said? Because that's exactly what it fucking sounded like, you fuck. I know exactly how you're being paid. You were paid three months before this speech. A rather secret Swiss bank account. Five million US dollars to give a speech, and schmooze with these blood-sucking bastards all weekend. You think that's a fair price? What's that as an hourly rate, sir? I'll tell you what it is. It's far more than I'll ever earn in a hundred lifetimes. I fought for my country. I went to war with people I've never met. And you know what I came back to? Nothing! No gratitude. No love. No money. No respect. You know how many friends of mine died in shitholes out there?"

The ex-president said, "I'm begging you ..."

Cain pressed the barrel of the gun tight to the ex-president's neck. The carotid artery was pulsating. He turned and faced the Secret Service man. "Drop your weapon or he dies. I'm going to count to five. And then he's gone. Make your choice."

The sirens wailed.

The Secret Service agent got to his feet and took a step forward. "You will do what I say. Drop the goddamn weapon! Now! There's no escape!"

Cain began to laugh. He leaned in close behind

the ex-president. He slid the barrel slowly under the man's right arm. Then he fired. The agent fell to the ground, clutching his shoulder as the gun fell out of his hand.

Cain stared at the guy for just a second. Then he pulled the trigger. Blood and gray matter splattered off the beige walls.

The ex-president collapsed to the ground, clutching his chest.

Cain began to smile. He ripped off his beard and threw away the glasses. He leaned down and hauled the ex-president to his feet. "Helluva day, huh?"

FORTY-THREE

As he bounded up to the fourth floor, Jon Reznick could hear the threats and shouts from Cain amid the fog of smoke and din of fire alarms. He peered through a glass door and squinted. The Florida sun was flooding through the windows. His brain was racing.

Think, goddamn it, think.

The memory of the ex-president pleading for his life, sobbing, and begging Cain for forgiveness, cut into him like a knife.

Reznick's earpiece crackled into life.

"Jon, where the hell are you?"

Reznick pressed his mouth to his cuff. "Fourth floor. Ex-president about to be killed." He leaned over and cracked the door. He sensed Cain was close to the stairwells. He craned his neck through the door and looked right. Twenty yards down the corridor Cain was laughing as he dragged the handcuffed ex-president through a fire-escape door.

Fuck.

"Be advised," Reznick whispered, "Cain heading

to the stairs on the north side of the fourth floor. Handcuffed to ex-President Adamson."

The earpiece crackled. "Jon?" The voice of Meyerstein. "Jon, Assistant Director Meyerstein. We copy that. You have full authorization to do what you see fit. I repeat, *full authorization*. SWAT are headed up the stairs on the north side. They're on the second floor."

Reznick made a mental calculation. "They've got that covered. I'm headed up."

He ran down the corridor and through the doors. Higher up the stairs came the sound of footsteps, panting and sobbing.

Reznick bounded up the stairs two at a time. "He's on five! But I think he's headed higher."

The earpiece static whistled in his ear. "Repeat, take down Cain!"

Reznick headed higher. Senses switched on. Dark thoughts crowded his head. He pushed them aside. He was back in the zone. The seconds were counting down.

FORTY-FOUR

Hunter Cain was breathing hard as he dragged the handcuffed ex-president to a fire-exit door on the sixth floor. He pulled the handle. Locked. "Fuck." He shot off the lock and pushed it open. Harsh sunlight flooded in. He headed out on to the roof of the complex. Views of Fisher Island. Biscayne Bay and the skyscrapers of downtown Miami in the distance. "Wow, now this is nice, huh?"

The target was sobbing hard. "Please ... I have no idea who you are, or what your grievances are."

Cain grabbed the target by the hair and dragged him to the edge of the roof terrace. He looked down and saw cop cars and dazzling lights down below. "Bit of a crowd already."

"Please, I beg you. I have a wife, children. Grandchildren."

"You know what I have? Nothing. I have no wife. No family. No anything. Do you think that's fair? Well, do you?"

Ex-President Adamson bowed his head, as if resigned to his fate. "Please ... son, I'm begging you ..."

"I ain't your son, you fuck. You corrupt fuck. You think you represent me? You think you represent America? The *real* America? Well, listen to me. *I'm* the real fucking America." Cain took off his tie with his free hand and ripped open his shirt, partially exposing the Semtex vest strapped to his tattooed torso. He flicked a switch on the front, connected to a cellphone and battery inside the vest, and a red light flashed on.

The ex-president glanced round and saw what Cain had strapped to his body. He closed his eyes and began to pray.

Cain pressed the gun to his head. "Praying ain't gonna save you. Praying ain't saved no one. You ever seen anyone blown up by a suicide vest, Mr President? No, I don't suppose you have." He pulled the cellphone out of his pocket, pressed a button and began to film himself and his victim. "This is gonna go viral like you wouldn't believe, bro." He began to laugh, cackling maniacally. "This is a great day to die, ain't it?"

FORTY-FIVE

The sound of laughing seeped through the partially open rooftop door. Jon Reznick peered out and saw the dire situation. He pulled back from the door. He looked up and squinted as the fierce sunlight streamed through a skylight above. His mind raced.

"Meyerstein, are you there?" he whispered into his cuff.

"Yeah, Jon. SWAT are fanning out."

"Please be aware, Cain is handcuffed to the ex-president and wearing a suicide vest."

"Goddamn."

"I need bolt cutters."

"Hold the line, Jon." A few moments later. "Jon … bolt cutters with Team B."

"What?"

"Long story."

"We haven't got time. Almost certainly already set on a timer."

"Jon, full authorization to do the necessary. Right now."

"Got it."

Reznick saw piles of tables and conference chairs

in the corner. He pulled out a table and put a chair on top. He clambered up and reached for the steel frame of the skylight. Then he pulled himself up and peeked over the edge. He was located ten yards diagonally behind Cain. He needed to shoot from a particular angle, or Cain would inadvertently pull his captor over the edge.

He hoisted himself up onto the roof terrace. Cain's wild ranting was in the ex-president's face.

Reznick aimed at Cain. He needed to be sure. Suddenly Cain spun round, the look of a cornered animal in his eyes. In that second, memories flooded back through Reznick's head. This was the man he had fought with. He stared at his friend for a split second.

Time seemed to stop. He felt the cold metal of the trigger. Pulled it twice. Two bullets ripped into the forehead. Blood erupted from the wounds.

Cain slumped to the ground and fell backward. His limp body began to drag Adamson towards the edge.

Reznick ran across the roof terrace and grabbed the ex-president by the arms, pulling him back to solid ground. He looked down at Cain, saw blood spilling from his mouth. He turned to face Adamson. "Sir, I need you to focus and do exactly as I say."

The ex-president just nodded.

"Firstly, do not move."

Reznick reached under his jeans and pulled out a

knife strapped to his calf. He bent over and cut Cain's shirt off him. The Semtex suicide belt was fully exposed.

Reznick said, "See what I'm talking about?"

Adamson nodded.

Reznick checked the suicide belt and saw the primitive trigger-switch that activated the belt. He tried to turn it off but it stayed on red. It was clearly battery-operated. "Fuck!" It could explode at any time.

He cut off the belt and threw it over the edge, onto a grassy area down below. "Meyerstein, suicide belt cut off and located in the parkland area below. Do you copy?"

"We copy that, Jon. Good work."

"He was going to manually detonate it."

Reznick saw that the ex-president was wearing a tiepin, still attached to his tie. He reached out. "Mind if I take this?"

"Go right ahead."

Reznick unclipped it and began to rub it on the stone at the edge of the roof till it became thin and sharp. He inserted it into the tiny hole in the hand-cuff lock and began to delicately jimmy it. He pressed his ear up against the cold cuffs as he listened to each turn. Eventually he felt the required point of the internal locking mechanism, and turned the tiepin sharply. A click, and the handcuffs were prized open. He extricated Adamson's chafed wrist from the handcuffs and escorted him back through the doors, where two SWAT guys had arrived at the scene. "They'll take you away from here, sir."

The ex-president looked long and hard at Reznick. "Who are you?"

"Sir, forget about me. We need to get you to a secure location." Reznick cocked his head at the two SWAT guys. "Get him out of here!"

Reznick turned and headed back onto the roof. A chopper with a SWAT team was overhead now, a sniper aiming down. The downdraft was making the operation difficult. He rifled in Cain's pockets and found a picture of Hunter as a boy, with his mother and father at the beach.

He turned over Cain's body, blood still oozing out of the two bullet wounds. Reznick stared down at the corpse of his old Delta buddy. He looked down below and saw a cordon was already set up.

A SWAT guy walked up. "We got it from here, Jon."

Reznick stared down at Cain again. He thought back to Fallujah. He thought back to the crazy, tough-as-nails warrior he knew. Then he thought of Cain's terrified girlfriend, assassinated on Cain's orders.

He sensed someone was watching him. He turned and saw Meyerstein walking towards him. She surveyed the scene.

"What a mess!"

Reznick nodded.

"But it could've been worse. A lot worse."

Reznick stared down at Cain.

"You okay?" she said, looking at him.

"We got blindsided on this."

"This was an elaborate, complex, operation," she said. "It must have been months, maybe years, in the making. And for what?"

"It was also a failure on our part. Lives have been lost. We didn't join up the dots." He shook his head. "What a fuck-up."

Meyerstein's earpiece crackled into life. She nodded. "Completely deactivated?" She paused. "Get it to Quantico labs for testing. We need to know where this batch was sourced from. Get back to me asap." She looked at Reznick again, walked to Cain's body and peered over the edge of the multistorey. Forensics were already photographing the discarded suicide belt. "Semtex?"

"Someone got hold of it. Ex-KGB are known to have access to stocks."

Meyerstein nodded. "What do you think Cain was going to do with Adamson?"

Reznick pointed to the cellphone on the ground. "Film him being killed for posterity."

"Chrissake!"

Reznick blew out his cheeks. "Are we done here?"

Meyerstein nodded. "You're done here. I've got a month of reports waiting for me. We'll need to investigate – who was pulling the strings? And there's a distinct possibility I might be kicked out of the FBI."

Reznick flashed a wry smile. "That ain't gonna happen."

"Why you so sure?"

"The FBI are many things, but stupid ain't one of them. You'll get a rap on the knuckles, and be told not to fraternize with guys like me."

"Yeah, if I'm lucky."

Reznick said nothing.

"Where you headed?" she asked, looking him in the eyes.

"Might go back to New York and finish that drink of mine."

"And after that?"

"Been offered an interesting job out in the Middle East."

"You gonna take it?"

"We'll see."

Meyerstein smiled.

"What about you?" he asked.

Meyerstein curled some hair behind her ear. "What about me?"

"Business as usual?"

"Well, firstly, I'll have to head straight back to DC and have a chat with the director."

"And then?"

"And then I'll go home, and shut the door, and see my kids."

Reznick said nothing.

"Will you be available in the future?" she said, her eyes fixed on him again.

"Why?"

"I need to know. In case the director asks."

Reznick sighed. He stared out at the water in the distance. "Tell him I'll think about it."

About the Author

J.B. Turner is the author of the acclaimed Jon Reznick action thriller series: *Hard Road*, *Hard Kill*, *Hard Wired* and *Hard Way* (Thomas and Mercer). The fifth book in the series, *Hard Fall*, is due for release in early 2018. He is also the author of the forthcoming Nathan Stone thriller, *American Ghost*, which is due for release some time in 2018, as part of a new thriller series. Turner also penned the Jon Reznick novella, *Gone Bad*, and the Deborah Jones crime thrillers, *Miami Requiem*, and *Dark Waters*. He began his writing career as a journalist. He is married and has two young children.

Check out his website at www.jbturnerauthor.com

Follow him on Twitter @jbturnerauthor

YOUR FREE BOOK IS WAITING

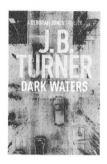

"How far would you go to uncover the truth"

When the partially dismembered body of a young man is found in the Florida Everglades, Deborah Jones, the fearless African American investigative journalist for the Miami Herald, finds herself caught up in a story that has ramifications for beyond anything she could have ever imagined. The victim had contacted Deborah anonymously just the day before, promising the top-secret government documents – the missing 28 pages of the 9/11 report – if she'd agree to a meeting. But he didn't show up, calling to say he feared for his life. Deborah Jones is a woman not easily deterred by threats. But when a second person dies in mysterious circumstances, it is clear to her and to everyone on her newspaper that Deborah could be next on the assassin's list.

Get your free ebook at:
www.jbturnerauthor.com

Printed in Great Britain
by Amazon

77757313R00119